TEXAS COWBOY JUSTICE

BARB HAN

TORJAKE PUBLISHING

Copyright © 2019 by Barb Han

All rights reserved.

No part of this book may be reproduced in any form or by any electronic or mechanical means, including information storage and retrieval systems, without written permission from the author, except for the use of brief quotations in a book review.

Editing: Ali Williams

Cover Design: Jacob's Cover Designs

For my family. I'm so fortunate to get to do life with each of you. My love for you has no bounds and I count my blessings every day.

1

Noah Quinn rolled out of bed and onto the wood floor of his cabin. He fired off a couple dozen push-ups as Callie, his nine-year-old border collie, trotted over.

Licking his face while he did his level best to finish his workout without dog slobber on his cheek had become sport. Callie usually won that fight, and this morning was no exception.

The cold morning took a bite out of Noah and he wished he'd put another log on the fire before hitting the sack last night. Noah did cold about as well as fish did land. The forecast had called for the cold snap to arrive closer to lunch, not before three-thirty a.m., his usual wake-up time. So now he had cold, wet saliva to look forward to as he spun onto his back and moved onto crunches.

Even though his routine hadn't changed since Callie came to live with him as a six-week-old pup, he'd done his level best to make it clear this was his workout not her playtime. Clearly, he'd lost that battle before it started because she lowered her head over her front two paws and wagged her tail hard enough to clear a coffee table. Her tail-wagging antics were precisely the reason Noah didn't have one of those.

The cabin didn't have much in the way of furniture or décor, for that matter. Noah had simple tastes. If he spent more time inside he might be bothered by the fact there were no pictures on the walls despite having lived here for more years than he cared to count.

All he needed was contained within these walls; a small kitchen, a bathroom and a living room with a sleeping nook. He owned a couch, a bed and a dinette set. His table for two had one too many chairs for his lifestyle. He'd kept it around in case he had company; since 'in case' turned out to be 'never', he'd considered ditching a chair to make extra room for Callie's bed. Call him a hopeless romantic but he'd kept the chair.

A couple dozen jumping jacks later, he walked over to the bathroom sink and brushed his teeth. A fresh pot had already brewed by the time he wandered into the kitchen, the requisite fresh mug to make him feel like a new man. Thank the stars for a few pieces of technology. The rest he could do without, like cell phones and tablets. Besides, his were useless where he lived on the ranch. No one was getting any connection out here.

While his bread was cooking in the toaster, he refreshed Callie's water bowl and heated her breakfast. He'd spoiled her, mixing wet food with her kibble. She was worth the extra energy and expense. A good cattle dog was worth three men, and besides, Callie was so much more than that.

Noah bent down and scratched her behind the ear, her favorite spot. He moved to his closet and pulled out the first warm thing he could find, a hoodie. He shrugged it on, fighting the shiver from the cold.

Tonight, he'd remember to put that extra log on the fire. At some point in the night Callie had made her way onto his bed and curled up next to his legs. Usually, that was a no-no. But since she only did it when the temperatures hovered above freezing, he couldn't get too upset with the little rule-breaker. Hell, if it got much colder tonight he'd grab the extra blanket and call Callie up so she wouldn't have to wait until he fell asleep to sneak on.

By the time he'd downed a second cup of fresh brew and finished his breakfast, it was four a.m. Life on his family's ranch started early. His father held a meeting in the barn every morning at this time.

No thanks had been Noah's long-standing policy to anything involving his formerly abusive father. But T.J. had recently called his sons home and was expected to make an announcement when the whole family was under one roof again. Another miracle in and of itself.

Thanks to T.J.'s live-life-on-his-terms policy, that hadn't happened since his older twin brothers, Isaac and Liam, had turned legal age to make their own decisions. Isaac had signed up for the military. Liam had gone to work at a ranch in Colorado. One by one, the rest of the Quinn brothers followed suit.

Of seven brothers, Eli and Noah were the only two who'd stayed on at the ranch. Noah's only condition was that he not have to attend T.J.'s morning meetings. Eli had made a habit of filling Noah in. But ever since T.J. had made the request for his sons to come home, speculation as to what his big announcement would be was running wild.

"Come on, girl." Noah made kissing noises. Callie darted across the floor. Even at her age, she still acted like a pup. "Ready?"

Callie ran circles around him, same as she had for nine years. As far as Noah was concerned, she needed to live forever; she'd been his right hand for too much of his adult life. He grabbed the keys to his Jeep from the hook next to the door, Callie circling his legs again. He opened the door and the wind blasted right through his hoodie as she eagerly ran outside. Damn.

Noah retrieved a coat from his closet. He shrugged it on and walked outside. Callie was probably taking care of business and that was most likely the reason he hadn't spotted her. Her black-and-white coat normally stood out against the early spring foliage. April in Texas meant experiencing all four seasons, sometimes in the same day.

His cabin was the furthest from the main house. Noah liked the feeling of living on his own with no one around for miles. Besides, he had the added benefit of keeping an eye out for illegal poachers; no one expected a cabin this rustic to be lived in full-time. He'd caught his fair share because he knew the land better than anyone, including T.J.

"Here, girl." Noah surveyed the area. No sign of Callie yet. If she took much longer, he'd miss Eli. Since Noah recently lost his phone, he couldn't exactly call for today's assignment.

The damn phone hadn't turned up. He hated the thought of buying a new one. Programming in his settings took more time than he cared to stare at a screen. Plus, spring on a cattle ranch gave him zero downtime. Busy wasn't a good enough word to describe life this time of year.

"Callie, where'd you head off to?" He whistled. That was the surefire way to get her attention. She should be running around the corner of the house any minute.

Noah hopped down from the porch. He didn't take two steps before Callie barreled toward him from the scrub bushes. "What were you doing over there?"

It wasn't like her to wander off. Could be an animal. Or poachers. This far in the thicket where his home was located brought him face-to-face with both.

"You hearing me okay?" Noah had noticed his best and favorite dog slipping lately. He kept a close watch on her. Her serious stink-eye still managed to keep the heifers in line when they tried to take her on. And retiring her wasn't even a question. He'd walk alongside her if he had to because she lived to work side-by-side with him.

The hairs on the back of his neck pricked. That prickly feeling of being watched, honed by years of tracking some of the most dangerous men, had him taking a second look at the trees. Instinct had Noah reaching for the pistol holstered at his back in the waistband of his jeans.

Callie trotted over to the truck as Noah surveyed the area.

Satisfied whatever had caught her attention had moved on, Noah walked over to his vehicle before opening the door. Callie immediately jumped in looking every bit the pup he hoped she'd stay. She claimed her usual spot in the passenger seat.

Almost half an hour later, he pulled up next to the barn and parked. The foreman leaned against the barn, his amused look indicated Noah was in for some ribbing.

"Your timing is impeccable," Dakota teased. "Meeting ended five minutes ago."

"I almost missed my grand entrance. A small animal or something caught Callie's interest in the thicket."

Dakota Viera shot a warning look. "I haven't heard of any poachers in your area. We'll keep watch just the same."

"Good to keep our eyes peeled."

"You should've called it in."

"Still can't find my damn cell." Noah figured his phone wasn't coming back. He'd hoped it would show up. Not being the keenest on having an electronic device glued to his hand, he'd put off replacing it. Besides, it wasn't like he got cell service in the parts of the land he most frequented. Another of many things to appreciate about being on the land for his job instead of inside a building.

There were plenty of others, like a sky that seemed to go on forever. More stars than he could count in one lifetime. A daily dose of fresh air.

Dakota dragged a glove over his right hand. "Since you weren't there to defend yourself—"

"What did I get nominated for this time?"

"Feed store run," Dakota said. "I can take Callie with me. She'll want to check on Cody if she hasn't already."

A feed store run definitely meant pulling the small straw. Since he refused to attend meetings, he'd found himself volunteered for more mundane tasks than he wanted. He didn't argue, though. He wanted to swing by and see if Mikayla Rae Johnson was working at the gas station this morning.

"Do I get a shopping list this time?"

"I'll text it to...well, hell, you already said your phone never showed up. What about a replacement?"

"Nope. Haven't had a chance to pick one up, either."

"They sell 'em at practically every convenience store." Dakota patted his coat pocket. "Got mine at the Easy-Mart."

"I'll keep that in mind."

Dakota made a sour face. "Just the thought of mine going missing for more than a day makes me squirm."

"You've gotten too used to modern conveniences, Dakota. Next thing you know, you'll be espousing the wonders of indoor plumbing."

This time, Dakota laughed.

For all T.J.'s faults, he knew how to put good people around him. Dakota and Marianne had worked for the Quinn's for as far back as Noah could remember.

Out of the corner of his eye he saw Jess Pacheco making a beeline in his direction. Before Noah got saddled with the greenhorn, he dug keys out of his pocket. "Call the order in."

"Already did." Sounded about right. Leave it to Dakota to use any chance he could get to needle Noah about not buying a new cell phone the minute his disappeared. The man had been running the barn at Quinnland Ranch since before Noah could recite the alphabet.

Dakota knew what he was doing. He might come in a few inches shorter than Noah but he wouldn't want to meet the man in a dark alley for the first time. Rumor had it that he and T.J. met in county lockup as teens.

The two apparently hit it off. So, when T.J. decided to get his life together and put together a future, he promised to find Dakota and give him a job. Dakota was back in lockup when T.J. bought his first piece of land. He'd picked it up from a widower whose family apparently had no idea she owned mineral rights or they probably would've tied up the land in court.

T.J. had gone to work for the Orlin widow as a teenager. He credits her with helping him sort out his life. Then, she'd surprised him by selling him the property in her will for seven dollars. Folks had since made a sport of speculating how he'd convinced her to do it.

According to T.J., he had no idea about her plans. She'd told him to wait patiently for a year before he did anything. Once the case was out of probate, he'd staked his claim and started building his empire. In less time than it took to age a decent bottle of scotch, T.J. had made his first million. Apparently, like the old saying went, the second one had been a lot easier.

"I'll be back. Have someone ready to help unload the truck this time." Noah took off at a light jog toward the vehicle.

Dakota chuckled. He'd been on the straight and narrow path for thirty-five years. Made a damn respectable man out of himself. He lived by two rules. Never miss a meal. And never miss an opportunity to play a good prank.

If anyone knew what T.J.'s big announcement was going to be, it was Dakota. One of his best traits was loyalty, so there'd be no getting the information out of him.

Noah piled into the driver's seat before greenhorn Jess could catch up. The kid was sweet but a little too eager at times. Dakota said the kid was star struck by Noah. If he was in the barn, or hell, any room the kid turned his full attention to Noah.

Dakota was a good mentor and would keep the kid busy. Noah continued down the long drive.

A stab of guilt nicked him. Damn. The kid had had a rough upbringing, not unlike Noah's. Apparently, Jess had witnessed something traumatic though no one was certain what he'd seen. His father had been arrested when he was young, something like twelve-years-old and Jess had been passed around the foster care system for one reason or another.

Noah made a mental note to spend a little more time around Jess. He'd had it rough and, as Dakota had put it, could use as many positive male role models as possible. Noah wasn't so sure about being a role model to anyone, let alone Jess. But, hell, he was willing to give it a try.

It was still dark outside. Despite daylight savings time turning the clock forward the sun wouldn't be up for another couple of hours. The deer whistler on the truck should warn any strays to stay off the road. Noah was protective over all animals and especially against human inventions, like automobiles.

He navigated off the property and onto the farm road leading into town. This morning had his mind churning. He'd had a bad run-in with a poacher last month who'd threatened to reach out from prison to exact revenge. And yes, Nick Harlingen had been arrested and was locked up in jail, his threat idle, but maybe Harlingen was the reason for Noah's bad feeling earlier.

Noah couldn't shake the feeling something was off. It was just shy of five a.m. and it was already shaping up to be a day.

A vehicle caught his attention. Mikayla's? What was her car doing parked at Russell Lake this time of the morning?

Granted, for some this was still the night before. And Mikayla had made it clear at the coffee shop the other week that she wanted nothing to do with him. She didn't show at Isaac's wedding where Noah had planned to ask her what he'd done wrong.

She could be stranded. He turned into the lot and navigated toward her unmistakable two-door convertible. Her vehicle was cobalt blue, her favorite color. And after seeing the same in her eyes, it had become his favorite, too.

Her tires had air. No one appeared to be in the vehicle. He shouldn't let it bother him that she would meet up with someone else at the very spot the two of them had met up the couple of times they'd gone out.

He pulled up next to the driver's side and got out. The prickly feeling that made the hairs on the back of his neck stand on end returned.

MIKAYLA RAE JOHNSON tried to scream. She couldn't make much noise with masking tape covering her mouth. For the last hour she'd been trapped in the back of some...*thing*. She had no idea what it was or where she was. Her heart pounded against her ribs in painful stabs. She struggled against the bindings on her wrists.

One minute, she was answering a text from Noah Quinn and the next thing she knew he'd convinced her to meet him at their usual spot. His Jeep was nowhere to be seen when she parked at the lake and that should've been her first clue something was off. *He* was off.

The next thing Mikayla knew, the back of her head was met with blunt force. She momentarily blacked out. And now she was locked in some metal box too small to be the back of a semi and too big to be a crate.

Best she could tell she was alone. Noah was gone. For how long?

2

Mikayla was nowhere in sight. Her car door was unlocked. Keys were still in the ignition. The prickly sensation that had been stalking him hit like a slugger on the practice field. Her purse was normally stashed in the floorboard of the back seat.

Noah opened the back door. The black leather handbag with fringe Mikayla usually had strapped over her shoulder stared back at him. *Damn.*

No woman wanted a man rummaging through her purse. Under different circumstances, Noah would be the last person to invade someone's privacy. This situation called for desperate measures.

The thought occurred to Noah that he might be trampling all over a crime scene. His brain couldn't fathom it, couldn't accept the possibility anything bad could've happened to Mikayla.

There'd been recent crime in Gunner, which was a shock for the small tightknit ranching community. Regina 'Gina' Anderson had moved back to town with her daughter, Everly, and a few days after being back while on a morning jog, Gina had unwittingly come across a murder scene. A friend they'd gone to high school with by the name of Brittany Darden had been murdered by her stepfather after he propositioned her. She'd refused. He'd murdered her in cold blood and then tried to erase Gina after she happened upon the scene.

Bo Stanley, the murderer, was locked up, the town ready to go back to normal, and Noah couldn't accept the idea Mikayla had been abducted. Or worse.

Noah poured the contents of Mikayla's purse onto the back seat, sifting through to find her phone. He set aside a small notebook and pen, her wallet and earbuds. Her sunglasses were still inside their case. There was gum, loose change and ChapStick. An already opened invitation to his brother's wedding was in there, too. She'd skipped the ceremony. No doubt because of Noah.

No cell phone.

It was most likely the fact that Noah had a cousin for a sheriff and two others who were U.S. Marshals causing his mind to go to some dark places. Mikayla wouldn't leave her purse in the backseat, keys in the ignition and door unlocked. Not even in Gunner and especially since the murder.

Folks might leave keys in their vehicle and the door unlocked if they ran into the post office or the grocery. Even a woman least aware of the possibility of crime would keep her purse with her. Noah scooped her belongings in his two hands and placed them back inside her handbag.

He thought of a possible scenario that didn't end up with her somewhere dead in a ditch. She met up with someone who needed her help. She hopped in the person's car without thinking about her personal belongings. They had to take off in a hurry.

The holes in that story could make cheese out of milk.

Another scenario weighed on his mind. This one involved her being taken against her will. He checked for any signs of struggle. Her purse had been where he'd expected it. Her car door had been closed. The recent murder helped him realize if something had happened to Mikayla she most likely knew the person.

He needed to get to a phone and call his cousin Griff, the sheriff. A quick scan of the rest of her vehicle revealed her cell wasn't there, either. It was too early for anyone else to be on the roads. For the first time since losing his, Noah regretted not having a cell on hand. Even he could appreciate something about modern technology. Phones turned out to be damn handy in an emergency.

Speaking of which, he might be able to clear up this situation with one call. Fine, he'd convinced himself to replace his. Now, it was time to take care of—

Ring tones broke the silence.

He sure as hell knew they couldn't be coming from him. He glanced around, searching for the culprit. The noise wasn't coming from far. He backed up, shut the car door and listened.

Noah dropped down to all fours. The sound was coming from underneath Mikayla's sedan. He flattened himself against the concrete and reached his arm under her vehicle. He closed his fingers around her cell and checked the screen.

The incoming call was from Mikayla's mother. Noah swiped right. "Mrs. Johnson, this is Noah."

"Oh. Noah." The woman sounded as confused as she would be considering she thought she was about to speak to her daughter.

"I apologize if I scared you."

"Surprised is a better word. How are you, Noah?" Mrs. Johnson had always been a kind soul. She'd been a single mother for as long as he could remember. She'd owned and managed the gas station by the highway for as long as he could remember. Ranchers, bakers, and highway gas station owners kept the same hours.

"I'm concerned about your daughter." He saw no reason to beat around the bush with small talk. If Mikayla was in trouble, this was a lifeline he didn't plan to squander.

"Did something happen?" Her mother sounded even more confused now.

"That's what I'm trying to figure out. On my way to the feed store, I saw her car parked near the lake." He didn't feel the need to mention he'd wanted to drive by his and Mikayla's old spot because he was dealing with a bout of nostalgia. It wasn't too far out of the way. "Her keys are in the ignition, her purse is in the back and she's nowhere to be seen." He also didn't mention the fact he'd just found her cell underneath said car. He didn't want to overload her with information if there was an easy explanation.

"Oh. That doesn't sound like Mikayla at all." She paused like she needed a few seconds to let the information sink in. "She was scheduled to work with me this morning and didn't show. I haven't heard from her since yesterday. She stopped by for supper last night. I got worried that maybe her car broke down on the way in. She's been having trouble with it ever since it hit fifty thousand miles last month."

Noah didn't like the sound of this one bit. "There could be an easy explanation for this. Right now, I need to notify the sheriff." Dammit. He just remembered when this call ended he'd be locked out of her phone.

"I was just about to suggest doing the same. Will you call me back the minute you know anything?"

She probably wouldn't know, but he figured he had to ask anyway. "Do you, by chance, know the password to unlock her phone?"

"No, I don't. I'm sorry."

"This phone is useless to me once we hang up except for the ability to call 911. Can you call the sheriff for me? Let him know what I just told you and where I am. I'll stay here and walk the lake until he gets here." Most local folks had Griff's number programmed in and especially business owners who might need to reach him urgently. Gunner was the kind of place folks were on a first-name basis with each other and family businesses went back generations. The more reason Brittany's recent murder had been all that more shocking.

He hoped like hell Bo Stanley didn't have any family members who'd decided to show up in town and follow his lead. He'd confessed to killing his stepdaughter and to attempting to murder Noah's newly minted sister-in-law, Gina.

Noah walked to the truck, phone in hand. He needed a six-letter combination to unlock her cell. The answer to her disappearance waited right there and he couldn't touch it. The thought she might be lying in a ditch somewhere with minutes to live haunted him.

Pacing would do no good. He did it anyway.

Scanning the area for the fifth time would do no good. He did it anyway.

Going over the way she looked the last time he'd seen her would do no good. He did it anyway.

Fortunately for him, Griff barreled into the parking lot a few minutes later. Noah wasted no time bringing his cousin up to speed. He held out her cell phone.

"Let me retrieve an evidence bag. I don't want any more prints on there than we already have just in case." Griff made a good point. Noah had stupidly put his hands all over her phone. He hadn't thought, he'd acted. There wasn't much he could do about it now.

When Griff returned with a paper bag, Noah came clean. "My prints are going to be all over her car doors, her purse and now her cell. I wasn't thinking when I touched everything."

"We'll preserve what we can. You weren't expecting to come upon a possible crime scene. We aren't sure what we're dealing with just yet."

Noah shot his cousin a look.

"We don't have a twenty-hour waiting period to file a missing person's report if that's what you're worried about. I can start a search for her now. I'll get her description and last known whereabouts into the database and see if we get any hits."

"This isn't much to go on." Noah didn't have to work in law enforcement to realize the probability of getting a response was next to none.

"Hernandez is on his way over to process the scene." Deputy Larry Hernandez had been a childhood friend. He'd moved to Austin after high school before returning to Gunner with a pregnant wife last year. He and his wife, Cecily, had wanted to bring up their child in a safe town; Griff had hired him on the spot and from what Noah heard hadn't regretted bringing Larry on board for a second.

There wasn't much more Noah could do by sticking around. Standing around waiting for others to do a job while he looked on while twiddling his thumbs had never been his strong suit. "I'm going to stop by the Easy-Mart and pick up a phone after I leave here. I'll call Sherry and give her my number. Will you let me know if anything comes up?"

"You know I will." Noah brought his cousin into a bear hug. "I'll be in touch."

Noah climbed behind the wheel of the truck. The feed store was no longer on his radar. If he had to drive around all day, he would figure out a way to find her.

ON HER SIDE, Mikayla wiggled and strained until she sat upright. Her mind was still trying to wrap around the thought Noah Quinn could do something like this to her. She'd lived in the same town most of her life. He'd been a couple of years older than her in school, but she'd been around his family most of her life.

Of course, anyone who wasn't a Quinn was an outsider. To say the Quinn brothers were close was a lot like saying whales swam in pods. Granted, she didn't know Noah Quinn personally. He kept to himself mostly. But she'd never heard anything bad about him.

There were rumors about his father, T.J., and that the Quinns hadn't had as golden a childhood as some believed. Mikayla's mother had been friends with their longtime housekeeper, Marianne. Although Marianne never spoke ill of T.J. Quinn where Mikayla could hear, she had walked into her mom's kitchen more than once to sudden whispers, Marianne's expression intense.

The few times she'd gone out with Noah, he'd seemed polite and well-mannered. The man, like all his brothers, was the kind of good-looking that made people refer to a certain Kennedy. Tall, dark hair, chiseled features. Beautiful eyes. A body made for sin.

On top of that, Noah had been charming and easy to talk to. He could be funny. None of those traits had signaled *kidnapper* to her.

Noah had surprised her when he stopped by the gas station early one morning to ask her on a date. She'd had no idea he was interested in her to begin with. The first couple of times he suggested they go out she'd been busy. Nothing exciting but she had commitments. She'd been easing out of a relationship and hadn't wanted her ex to think she'd dumped him to go out with a Quinn.

Mikayla figured Noah would give up. But, no, he'd turned on the charm instead. When those sky-blue eyes were trained on her, she'd melted. Then there was his reputation as a playboy. Although, she'd never seen him with a different woman on his arm every other week, like some would have her believe. Still. It would only be a matter of time before he figured out that she was in over her head with him no matter how genuine and interested he'd seemed.

On the first date, coffee, they'd talked for two solid hours before she realized her drink had turned to ice. Iced coffee might be a thing for some people, but she liked hers warm. During the second date, lunch, he'd been just as charming. They'd stayed in town, eaten at a local restaurant. They had more in common than she realized. They both loved Texas, small towns, and lots of room between neighbors. She'd believed things were going well between them.

The only reason she was thinking about their history now was because she desperately needed to figure out how she'd misjudged the man so badly.

After the third day, he'd started with the texts. The first couple were confusing. The rest were just downright angry. She hadn't expected those, either. She'd tried to call him and straighten it out, but he sent her a demeaning text demanding that she leave him alone. He'd threatened to turn her in to his cousin for stalking him.

Talk about whiplash.

Angry, hurt, she'd vowed never to speak to him again.

And then she'd bumped into him at the grocery store and he'd pretended like nothing was wrong. Like he hadn't just toyed with her heart because he was handsome Noah Quinn and could get any girl in town.

Seeing him at the coffee shop the other day had made her see red. She'd had a good mind to walk over to his table and give him a piece of her mind, except that she'd seen a baby at the table. Stalking out of the coffee shop had seemed like a better idea at the time. Pride had her not wanting him to know just how much he'd gotten to her.

Damn his confused look, too. That almost had her question whether he'd sent her the texts in the first place. Her phone history didn't lie. She hadn't needed to re-read those messages to know what they said.

Damn that she'd only barely gotten to know him and he already had the power to trample on her heart.

Damn Noah Quinn.

Anger built inside her like a tsunami. There was no outlet. She kicked and the sound was deafening. The echo said she was in some kind of container. What? Like a moving pod?

The hum of an engine dragged her out of her revelry. Screaming would do no good. So, she banged on the container with the heel of her boots.

Please, someone, hear me.

She stopped the racket and listened. An engine was definitely idling nearby. *Please. Please. Please.*

This time, she banged her heels harder and tried to scream against the masking tape. Footsteps sounded outside the container.

A door opened and the crack let a little sunlight in. Panic tightened her chest when she got a good look at the man coming toward her.

Noah.

3

Mikayla screamed the second Noah removed the tape from her mouth. "Get away from me, Noah Quinn." Logically, it didn't add up that he was helping her take off the bindings, but emotions were in control at this point and she was straight-up freaking out after what he'd done to her last night.

"Be still so I can cut these damn ropes off without hurting you." His face was all business. Concern lines scored his forehead as he freed her legs first and then her wrists. He held up a wrist and examined the rope burn. He checked the rope again. "Damn it. Looks like the same kind we use from the feed store."

Mikayla scooted away from him, pain registering in her arms and ankles as the blood rushed to her extremities. "Don't get near me, Noah. I'll kick the living hell out of you."

The look of confusion he shot her next really had her questioning if she'd stepped into an episode of *The Twilight Zone*.

"What are you talking about, Mikayla?" His brows knitted together. "I'm here to help you and I'd like to get you out of this storage container and have you checked out by a doctor if you'll let me."

"Call Griff. Get the law here."

"I can't. I lost my cell and haven't had time to replace it."

Did she just hear him right?

"Where's your phone?"

"If I knew that it wouldn't be lost." If it wasn't for the sincerity in his expression, she'd scream for help. There didn't seem to be any vehicles around other than his family's truck. The hum of his engine was the first sound she'd heard since being locked inside the container last night.

"Where were you when you lost it?"

"Most likely on the ranch, but I can't honestly say for sure. You already know I'm not one for using it more than I have to." That part was true enough. The first time she'd offered to give her phone number to him he'd asked why he needed it. He'd said he knew where she worked and where her mother lived. If he needed to get a message to her that badly he had resources.

Mikayla had thought Noah was a refreshing change of pace. He had those old-fashioned manners some folks said were lost, like opening a door for her or refusing to let her chip in for the check. His smile was disarming. He had charm in spades. She didn't need someone to open the door for her or paying for her meal, but she enjoyed the offers. And especially on a date.

So, he'd been the last person she would feel in danger being around.

"How'd you find me?"

"I heard you. Now, let's get you in the truck." He offered his hand and she drew back.

Her heart thundered in her chest. Reason kicked in. He wouldn't have cut her loose if he meant to do her harm. None of this made sense, Noah abducting her was absurd, and she hadn't seen the person who hit her in the back of the head. If what he said was true about losing his phone, she could risk trusting him.

Then again, she was a little short on options.

Mikayla took the hand being offered, ignoring the electricity humming through her fingers from contact.

"Let's get you to safety."

Her ankles burned from the ropes, but she wasn't in there long enough to do any real damage. A headache threatened to split her skull in two. "I got a text from you asking to meet up last night. I refused after the way you'd been speaking to me. You said you'd explain your erratic behavior and I wanted to know what the hell was wrong with you."

Noah opened the door to the passenger side and offered a hand up. She climbed in. Shock that any of this could be happening was a force brewing inside her.

"I'm sorry that happened but I'm just as confused as you are. Needless to say, I never sent the text. I'm racking my brain trying to remember the last time I used my phone, coming up empty. Half the time, it's out of battery and I don't realize it." He turned the key in the ignition, put his hand on the gearshift, and faced her. "I can take you to the hospital or to Griff's office. It's your call."

"Home. Please. I want a hot shower and clean clothes."

Noah shot a questioning look. "The hospital might be a better choice. They have kits—"

"He didn't do anything physical to me aside from hitting me on the back of the head. I'm certain I don't need a rape kit if that's what you're thinking."

"He had to have dragged you into the storage container. His DNA might be on your clothes. I already trampled one crime scene. I'd like to protect evidence, so we get make sure this bastard is put behind bars."

"That's a good point. Once we get home, we can let Griff know. I won't change until he gets there. Just get me away from that thing." She pointed toward the storage POD and involuntarily shivered.

Thankfully, Noah punched the gas pedal and got her the hell out of there.

"We need to stop off and get a phone so we can call this in to Griff. He needs to get to the scene as soon as possible before evidence can be erased."

"As much as I want to get far away from here I realize you're right." She was getting her bearings and logic was kicking in.

"There's a convenience store a couple of blocks from here. Mind if we stop there?"

"Do I have to leave the truck?"

"No. I'll park in front where you can see me the whole time and we'll lock the doors. You can keep the engine running if you'd like."

She nodded. He was going out of his way to make her feel comfortable and she appreciated him for it.

"If you weren't the one who sent the texts, then who?"

"That's the sixty-four-thousand-dollar question." Noah pulled into the parking lot of the Easy-Mart. He parked in front of the double glass doors, just like he'd said. "Are you sure you're okay while I go inside?"

"Yes. Thanks for asking. And thank you for everything you've done for me so far." She couldn't imagine what might've happened if he hadn't shown when he did. "I'm sorry for accusing you."

"You're welcome and don't worry about it. Based on what you've said so far there was no reason to think otherwise." He didn't make a move to shut off the engine or take the keys. "Lock the doors as soon as I get out. Okay?"

She nodded.

"There's bottled water in the backpack behind the seat." He reached over and brushed the backs of his fingers against her cheek. "I'm sorry for what you've gone through. We'll find the bastard and make sure justice is served."

There was comfort in those words she couldn't afford to allow. But she did.

Mikayla pinched the bridge of her nose, waiting for Noah while he ran into the convenience store to buy a throwaway phone. The sun was too bright and made her head pound. A glance at the clock said it was half past ten in the morning. Her throat was dry. Nausea overwhelmed her, and her stomach threatened to empty its contents. Bile burned the back of her throat as she realized there wasn't much inside to vomit.

When Noah returned, she unlocked the vehicle for him, he immediately called 911 and requested to speak to Sherry, Griff's secretary. Noah put the call on speaker and then handed it to Mikayla.

"How can I help you, Noah?" The older woman's familiar voice came on the line and boomed through the speakers.

"Mikayla Rae Johnson is sitting in my truck. I'm parked at the Easy-Mart on Albany Circle."

Sherry gasped. "I'll get the sheriff on the line. Hold tight."

A few seconds later, Griff's voice filled the cab. "Where did you say you are?"

"Easy-Mart on Albany Circle but Mikayla would like to go home." Noah seemed to pre-empt the next question. "I found her in a storage POD at the old warehouse by the Storage Shack. She's lucid. You can speak to her if you'd like."

"Mikayla?"

"I'm here, Griff."

"Tell me everything you can remember about what happened?" He didn't have to tell her time was of the essence.

She gave him the quick run-down, figuring she could go into more detail once he arrived at her place. "Can I go home?"

"Other than the blow to the back of your head, he didn't hurt you in any way?"

"No. He didn't."

"Then, I don't see any reason you can't go home. I'll meet you there as soon as I can. Take off your clothes carefully and place them in a paper sack if you have one."

"I do and I will."

"One more thing. Giving your permission to check your phone will speed up the process—"

"Absolutely. You have my permission. Check my text messages."

"You'll find messages from my lost phone on there," Noah warned.

"How's that?"

"Someone must've found my cell and decided to use it…" It

seemed to hit Noah just how unlikely that was when he paused for a beat. "I'm guessing the chances my phone was lost is next to nil."

"Not a horse I'd bet on."

"Dammit to hell." Exactly the phrase Mikayla was just thinking.

"We'll need to file a theft report. We can talk more about it in person," Griff said.

She thanked him and ended the call.

Noah was already heading toward her place. He knew where she lived from when he'd picked her up before a date. She leaned her head back against the headrest and tried to process everything that had occurred in the past twelve hours.

"I saw you walk into the coffee shop last week. You took one look at me, turned around and walked out. I'm guessing the texts had already started by then and that was the reason for the about-face."

"You...*he*...whoever it was who took your phone, had called me a stalker. Told me not to get anywhere near you if I didn't want a restraining order filed."

"And you believed him?" The hurt in his deep timbre shouldn't chip away at the protective wall she'd erected. Nor should she allow his deep baritone to wash over her. Noah Quinn scared her. Not because she believed he'd whacked her in the back of the head and stuffed her in a container until he could come back and do whatever he wanted to her—she shivered at the thought of what might've happened if he hadn't come along when he did—but because she liked him.

"What made you come to this area?"

"I saw your vehicle and literally have been driving around for hours trying to figure out where someone would take you. Which reminds me, you should call your mother. She's worried sick about you since you didn't show for work this morning." He motioned toward the cell on the bench seat in between them.

"You spoke to my mother?" Oh no. Mikayla's poor mother would literally be sick from worry.

∼

MIKAYLA'S FACE twisted with distress. Noah couldn't help but want to reassure her. "We'll call her as soon as humanly possible. She called and that's how I found your cell. You must've had it in your hand while you were waiting for the person you were meeting." The person she thought was him. "It ended up underneath your car. I heard it ring and answered but couldn't access anything after the call without your password." What Noah had heard so far was enough to make his blood boil.

"You don't have any idea the last time you used your cell do you?"

"Not in the least. A few days ago? A week?" Remembering the last time he'd had his cell was like trying to keep track how many cups of coffee he drank in a day. Ask him where his keys were. He knew the answer to that question; keys were important to him. Ask him where any of the twelve fire extinguishers were located in the barn at any given time. He could rattle that information off at a pin drop; those were important to him. His mostly useless phone due to his lack of love for technology coupled with spotty cell service on the ranch property? Not so much.

"I don't recall what happened. One minute I'm standing outside my car waiting for you and the next I'm on the ground with a blindfold over my eyes. I couldn't have blacked out for more than a few minutes. My hands and feet were already tied when I came to. It took a minute to figure out what was happening and by that time I was being thrown onto the bed of a truck."

"One person? He acted alone?"

"There was only one set of hands lifting me."

Whoever did this was strong. Hearing what she'd endured sent firebolts shooting through Noah. It was more than the fact the perp had posed as Noah or the fact that someone he knew had been put in that situation, much more, but this wasn't the time to evaluate why that was.

Mikayla was as kind as she was beautiful. She had one of those smiles that made him realize the sun was out. Who could possibly want to hurt her? A few dark thoughts struck at what a creep might want to do with an attractive woman who was tied up. He pushed those aside, focusing on the one that mattered. "Why?"

Noah pulled onto her street and then into her driveway. He parked on the pad next to her white bungalow before helping her out of the truck. She'd refused to drink any water on the way over and he noticed that her face had paled. He figured the day was catching up to her and she was having trouble processing it.

He'd been around people who'd experienced trauma. Seen it with his family.

"I can keep watch for Griff while you change your clothes and clean up if you want." He'd only been in her house once before and he remembered thinking back then that the place suited her. The living room was painted a light beige color, her sofa beach-house white with pale blue throw pillows and all the light colors in the house gave the place a welcoming feel. Everything had a place.

This time he noted a small stack of books and another of magazines on top of the glass coffee table, a blue vase with fresh white flowers next to a matching blown-glass bowl. The swirls in the patterns reminded him of her eyes.

Her laptop was on the couch, still open.

"Are you sure you don't want to have some water?"

"It's probably a good idea." She moved to the sink and filled a coffee mug with water. She took a few sips.

"Make yourself at home." She returned from the kitchen holding a paper bag. "Excuse me while I change."

"Mind if I put on coffee?" He'd seen her coffee maker the last time he was here.

"Help yourself." She walked toward the hall and then paused. She turned. "I've had a rotten few hours and as much as it pains me to admit this, I'm afraid of my own shadow right now. Will you keep me company while I get dressed?"

Noah understood. He nodded, set his keys in the bowl and followed her down the hallway to her master bedroom. He was torn between his need to treat her with care and respect after the experience she'd had and his own physical reaction to a very beautiful Mikayla undressing a few feet away from him.

"Do you mind?" She motioned for him to turn his back.

Normally, turning his back on a room was the last thing he'd consider doing for safety reasons. In this case, with Mikayla, he made an exception.

Leaning against the doorjamb, he waited, forcing the thought Mikayla was about to be naked and in the same room with him out of his thoughts.

4

Since Noah wasn't thinking about the fact that Mikayla was standing about five feet behind him naked, he decided not to think about the first kiss they'd shared, too. And especially not the way her body had melted against him when his tongue had darted inside her mouth.

Their breath had quickened, pulses risen as those cherry lips of hers parted to give him better access.

He also denied the thought about how quickly he'd been aroused when her pert breasts were flush against his chest with a few layers of thin material between them. Then there was the fact that he'd brought his hand up to the base of her neck, his fingers tangled in her wheat-colored locks with curls for days and she'd moaned against his lips.

All those thoughts were inappropriate under the circumstances. So, with effort, he pushed them aside even though his body took its time following suit. He rested his shoulder on the doorjamb and waited. Thought about changing the oil in his Jeep and how his tires were due for rotating. Anything to keep his mind off those long runner's legs of hers or how soft her creamy skin had felt underneath his hands.

Noah was losing the battle.

"Ready." One word had never been so welcomed.

"I'll put on that fresh pot now." Noah didn't turn around. He didn't need the image of Mikayla in her bedroom stuck in his head. And he especially didn't need that image while looking into her cobalt blue eyes. "Griff should be here any minute."

True enough, Griff knocked before Noah set up the coffee. Mikayla stared at the door.

"Do you want me to answer?"

"Thank you." Those sincere blues hit him as he walked past. He took a shot to the heart but kept going when his arms wanted to take on a mind of their own and haul her against his chest. His mouth wanted to whisper reassurances and take her fear away. He chalked it up to overactive protective instincts.

"Come on in, Griff." Noah held the door open.

After a quick greeting, Griff got down to business.

"Would you like to sit?" Mikayla asked. She held out the bag of clothes.

Griff took a seat adjacent from the sofa after setting the bag on the glass table. He pulled out a pocket notepad.

"First things first." He turned to Noah. "You're already aware of the texts sent from your phone."

"Yes." The idea someone had used him to trap Mikayla sat heavy in the pit of his stomach. His lost cell phone had given someone an opportunity to get to her. Noah brought over two mugs and a bottle of water for Mikayla. He set one of the cups down in front of Griff. "I don't like the fact that someone used my mistake or carelessness to get to Mikayla. Could this person have been watching her for a while?"

Out of the corner of his eye, he saw Mikayla tense at the thought. The question needed to be asked even though he hated how it made her feel. He fought the urge to reach out to her, to take her hand and try to comfort her.

"There's one theory that someone took advantage of you losing your cell. The other is that someone stole your phone, knowing he could get to her."

"It has to be a man, right?"

"Based on the fact the person acted alone and was strong enough to carry Mikayla when she was dead weight points to a male." Griff picked up his notebook and pen.

"I couldn't see his face but he was strong." The memory put a bitter look on her face. "His arms were thick and he was tall, like Noah. I never doubted it was him if that helps."

"A few of these might sound like obvious questions. I have to ask them anyway," Griff said.

Mikala nodded.

"Have you fought with anyone recently? Even the most seemingly insignificant argument could be relevant."

"No one off the top of my head." She closed her eyes and tucked a loose tendril of hair behind her ear. "Let's see. I had to get on the Bowery boy for trying to steal a candy bar on Tuesday. He was pretty upset when he got caught. I think it was his first time to test the boundaries."

Griff nodded. "What was his reaction to you?"

"He apologized, called me ma'am a lot, which made me feel like he was talking to my mother or something." She opened her eyes and her cobalt blues landed on Noah.

"He didn't throw a fuss or make any threats?"

"No. He seemed pretty shaken up about it."

"How old is he?" Noah asked.

"Around fourteen." Mikayla's eyes lit up. "No way is he strong enough. He hasn't filled out yet. His older brother's in college. He's at A&M."

"I'll check with the family to see if he's home for any reason. Doubt it, but it's worth following up on." Griff jotted down *Bowery*.

The kid could've been traumatized enough to tell his older brother. Seth Bowery had caused just enough trouble in high school to question whether he'd get into college and his younger brother seemed to be following in his footsteps. At their core, they seemed like decent kids though Noah wasn't close enough to the Bowerys to really know. Noah had long since graduated by the time Seth made it to high school.

"Does anyone you can think of hold a grudge against you?" Griff asked.

She shot a look toward Noah. "I've had a few snide comments directed at me since I was seen out socially with a Quinn."

Noah tried to keep his temper in check. She shouldn't have to put up with that.

"From who?"

"The Bridget sisters for one. They came in the gas station the other day and made a few Cinderella cracks just loud enough for me to hear."

Adelle and Lacy Bridget had made it clear to Noah and, to be honest, a couple of his brothers when they'd been in town, that the two of them were available and interested. He and his siblings had taken it lightheartedly, as a joke. Seeing it play out this way wasn't funny.

"I'm sorry that happened to you." He meant it, too. He'd never thought of the consequences that might come on the other side of dating a Quinn.

Mikayla's cheeks flushed with embarrassment and it made her even more attractive, if that was even possible. Noah doubted it was. He was being truthful, though. He didn't like that she'd been razzed for dating him.

If he had anything to say about it, she'd go out with him again once this ordeal was settled and she was safe.

"Does anyone you know hold a grudge against you for any reason?" Noah seriously doubted anyone could. Mikayla was kind, intelligent, giving. Who could be upset with her?

"Had a couple of humdingers in high school with a few girlfriends." She cracked a small smile. "But, no. I can't think of anyone who'd want to hurt me or have me hurt. I live a pretty boring life by most people's standards." Again, her cheeks flamed and, again, she looked damn beautiful.

"What do you mean?" Griff asked.

"I work a lot of early mornings, so I'm usually in bed by nine o'clock."

"How about dating?" This time, Griff shot the apologetic look toward Noah.

"Most recently, I went out with Noah. Before that, I spent time with Bode Harding but I broke it off around the time I started seeing Noah." Suddenly, the bottle of water in her hands became real interesting.

Bode Harding? Sure, he was probably good-looking to most women.

"Didn't he move to San Antonio recently?"

"A month or so ago." She twisted off the lid and took a sip, not making eye contact with Noah.

He bowed his head and stared at the rim of his coffee mug, pretending not to be affected. The shot to the gut he took felt a little extreme considering he and Mikayla had only been out a handful of times.

"Did you cut off communication with him when he moved?" Noah stared harder at the ceramic.

"We keep in touch." Another right hook slammed into Noah.

"Are you still dating?"

Out of the corner of his eye, he saw her shrug. "If you ask me? No."

"And if I ask him?"

"He wanted to keep things going after he moved but I couldn't see the point. I'm here and he's there. We weren't far enough along into the relationship for me to consider going with him when he asked. Besides, Noah had asked me out." She stopped abruptly like she'd said too much.

"Did he ask you to move to San Antonio?"

"Yes." She shifted in her seat and then glanced up at Noah. That one look sent another shotgun blast straight to the center of his chest. He didn't like this conversation. Yet, he had no hold on her or her past. The two of them had barely gone on a few dates. They'd kissed.

And, although it had been one helluva kiss, it didn't mean they were exclusive. An annoying as hell voice in the back of his mind argued the opposite, saying a man knew when he'd met his match.

Since Bode had asked Mikayla to move to San Antonio with him after a few dates, he seemed to be pretty struck by her. His mistake had been trying to move their relationship forward faster than she'd been ready.

"Was Bode upset when you told him you wouldn't move?" Griff asked. Again, Noah tried not to care too much about the answer.

"Yes, but he said he'd convince me."

"Did he know you started seeing someone else?"

"We didn't talk about it but it's not like I was hiding the fact, either. It honestly never came up in our conversation." She pursed her lips together. "Hold on. Now that I think about it, he hinted that he realized something was going on."

Noah didn't like the picture emerging and Griff seemed to be on the same path based on his line of questions. It was possible that Bode didn't take the news as well as she thought. He could've been the one to steal Noah's phone and send her those messages, been the one to hit her on the back of the head and stuff her in the container POD. He might've been trying to scare her into thinking Gunner wasn't safe anymore. Or just flat-out trying to hurt her. God only knew what would've happened to her if Noah hadn't gotten there when he did.

Which also got him wondering why the abductor left her alone to begin with. Had he been interrupted? Or had he needed to get back to San Antonio?

"How did he sound?"

"Like he didn't like it at first. I made it clear to him that I wanted a break *for me*. He seemed to take it well after the idea had a little time to seed. Told me to take all the time I needed."

"Do you think he really meant it?" The question had to be asked.

Mikayla's face blanked.

~

"I believed him at the time. Now? I have questions. I'd like to think he wouldn't do anything so scary or drastic." Mikayla had seen a possessive side to Bode early on and that was one of many reasons she'd decided to back away graciously.

Honestly, they hadn't been going out long enough for him to become too jealous. As far as she was concerned there hadn't been any decision to make when he'd broached the subject of her moving to San Antonio. Her life was in Gunner.

"He might've gotten word you started seeing my cousin. Bode might've seen that as a threat and figured he had to act." Griff scribbled a few more notes. "But we're getting ahead of ourselves. I'll send a deputy to San Antonio to ask him a few questions. See where he's been the past twenty-four hours; if he can account for his whereabouts we'll consider him a low-priority suspect."

"You already know from looking at my phone but Bode texted the other day asking if I'd meet him for dinner. I told him I had plans." She didn't. She'd been too disappointed by Noah's supposed texts to see anyone.

The connection she'd felt in just a few dates with Noah had made her believe something special was happening between them. What? She had no idea. No one had made her feel like he did. He was his own presence in a room and the kiss that they'd shared had skyrocketed her to new heights—heights she'd never reached with another man. It had scared and intrigued her and one thing was certain, it got her attention.

She also knew she'd be measuring every other kiss against that one for the rest of her life. There'd been no fireworks display when she'd kissed Bode. Not so much as a spark. He wasn't especially bad at kissing and she thought he was decent at the time. Until Noah.

"Other than Bode and Noah, have you been seeing anyone else?"

"No, and I wasn't seeing those two at the same time." She wasn't sure why she felt the need to clarify the point. Griff's half-smirk told her she'd said it a little too quickly. Her cheeks flamed.

She hadn't needed the Bridget sisters to let her know she was out of her depth with Noah; her heart had already warned her of the trouble she could be in getting close to him.

"I'm sorry for the questions."

"Don't be. I overreacted just now. It's strange talking about my personal life like this, digging around for someone who might want to hurt me." She shrugged before taking another sip of water to give her an extra few seconds to collect her thoughts. "I would never hurt anyone on purpose, so the idea someone would want to hurt me is such a foreign concept. My family isn't especially wealthy. Don't get me wrong, we've been fortunate to have always had food on the table and clothes on our backs. But we aren't wealthy. It's not like someone could blackmail my mother into sending a million dollars for my safe return."

Glancing up at Noah was probably a mistake. She did it anyway and saw compassion instead of judgment.

"I have the same problem as you do. I can't for the life of me figure out who would want to hurt you." Noah's kind words warmed her heart. Again, she knew better than to touch the hot stove twice. And going out with him would be tempting fire.

"I don't party too hard or drink too much, which probably makes me the most boring person in the state of Texas. I like to read and spend time on my horse. I don't like people as well as I like animals, and that suits me just fine." She really was making herself out to be a killjoy. When she thought about her life in these terms, it wasn't very exciting.

So, she added, "I have friends." Or at least she used to. "Most of whom moved to bigger cities after college graduation. I stayed in Gunner to help run the family business, be near my mother and my horse. Plus, I love Texas. I can't think of a place I'd rather be than here, which also probably makes me sound pretty lame for not having grand plans of living in a big city."

She glanced up at caught Noah studying her. Since she couldn't read his expression anymore, she turned toward Griff.

"Do you have any other questions for me?"

5

Noah couldn't imagine having to expose details of his personal life to people he barely knew. Granted, he and Mikayla had been out on a couple of dates—dates that had been damn enjoyable—but probably made this line of questioning a whole lot worse.

Griff explained to Mikayla that he'd like for her to stay in town over the next few days. It was standard and he'd heard it before. Griff handed over his personal cell number and asked her to call if she remembered anything or had additional questions.

And then Griff turned to Noah. "Since your phone was used to bring Mikayla to the meeting spot, I have a few questions for you next."

Growing up around law enforcement, Noah had seen this coming. "Ask anything you need to."

"Where were you last night?" Griff shot an apologetic look even though the questions seemed like ones that had to be asked.

"At my cabin." No doubt Griff hoped for a better answer.

"Is there anyone who can verify your whereabouts?"

"Afraid not. I was there with Callie. It was just the two of us."

Normally, his answer would raise an eyebrow from an interviewer. Thankfully, Griff knew he wasn't capable of abducting Mikayla, but if another law enforcement agency got involved Noah couldn't expect the courtesy.

Mikayla raised an eyebrow.

"Callie's my cattle dog." The clarification caused the right corner of her mouth to upturn just enough to know she cared about the answer and was relieved he wasn't talking about another woman. Satisfied he'd allayed her fears, he turned back to his cousin. "You know what this time of year is like on a cattle ranch."

"I need to hear it in your words for my report." Right. There was that. Noah broke it down for his cousin in as few words as possible. Talking had never been his favorite activity. *Except with Mikayla*, an annoying voice in the back of his head pointed out. The two of them had talked for hours on their first date at the coffee shop. Time had zipped by and he hadn't wanted the date to end. Since then, he found that when something interesting happened in his day his first thought was to reach out to her.

"What about fights with anyone recently? Is there someone who might have a vendetta against you?"

"I've been too busy working to argue with anyone. I suppose we have a couple of greenhorns at the ranch and I may have gotten onto them a time or two. Nothing that came to blows, just giving them direction when they get off course. They're young; sometimes I have to raise my voice to get their attention. You remember what we were like at that age."

Griff nodded. Although they both knew that no Quinn ever strayed from the line too far. Not with T.J. and Uncle Archer around.

"No disagreements stand out in particular?"

"None that come to mind. Like I said, I've barely been off Quinnland property for weeks. That's what it's like in the spring calving season." The poacher would have nothing to do with this case.

"What about relationships?" Griff's gaze darted from Mikayla to Noah. "Are you seeing anyone other than Ms. Johnson?"

"No." For one thing, there wasn't time. And the other, dating for dating's sake, had lost its appeal a long time ago.

Again, the small smile returned and it only made Mikayla more beautiful when her eyes lit up. Jesus, the attraction he felt was magnet to steel.

Griff closed his notebook and returned it to his front pocket. He stood and picked up the bag of evidence. "We'll get these clothes processed and hopefully come up with a name. If you think of anything else, call me any time day or night."

Noah walked his cousin to the door, wishing the case could be solved that easily. "You know I will."

"Same goes for you, Mikayla." Griff paused at the door. "Do you have somewhere you can stay tonight? Or maybe have someone who can come over to be with you?"

"I'll work something out." Noah picked up on the slight tremor in her voice even though she cleared her throat presumably to cover it.

"My deputies will keep watch over your street. I'll do my best to keep someone in the area at all times."

"Thank you, Griff. That means a lot."

Noah shook his cousin's hand and then closed the door behind him. He didn't normally lock doors, so it felt out of place that he had the urge to for Mikayla's peace of mind.

"You haven't eaten since last night. Think you can get a few bites down?"

"Maybe after a shower." She pushed up to standing. "Is it okay if I leave the bathroom door open?"

"Not a problem. I'll keep my ears open. If it makes you feel any better, he's not coming back on my watch." It was a promise Noah had every intention of keeping.

"It does." Mikayla disappeared down the hallway and Noah made his way into the adjacent kitchen. He checked the fridge and found milk, cheese and half a dozen eggs, and towards the back there was a fresh-looking bag of spinach and a half-chopped onion.

Noah gathered up the ingredients, figuring he could make a

decent omelet out the supplies. He topped off his coffee mug while he was at it. The shower kicked on while he located a knife and chopped the onion. He found a mixing bowl in the cabinet and whipped together the meal by the time the water from the bathroom cut off.

There was bread on the counter next to the toaster, so he made quick work of toast and when Mikayla bounded into the room, he had quite the table set.

"If I'd known breakfast was going to smell this good, I'd have hurried up." Her face lit up when she smiled and his chest nearly burst from pride from being the one to put it there. She'd been through hell and back in the past twenty-four hours. Lightening her mood felt damn good.

"If you want to sit, I'll bring over a plate." He ignored just how well her yoga pants fit her hips and the thin strip of skin visible from the T-shirt hem that didn't quite reach the waistband of her bottoms. Her wavy hair was piled on top of her head in a loose bun. His fingers itched to do away with the rubber band and let her hair fall around her shoulders.

Noah put the plate of food down in front of her along with a fresh cup of coffee.

"I'm not kidding, this not only smells amazing but it looks even better. Where did you learn to cook like this?"

"Living alone helps. Marianne taught me a few things before I moved out of the main house, which I couldn't do fast enough for my taste. I picked up the rest along the way."

She mewled after taking the first bite.

Noah shook his head, turned around and walked toward the sink.

"Where's your food?" she asked. "Aren't you joining me?"

"I can." Noah fixed his own plate and took a seat across from her at the table.

She studied his face as she took her next bite. "Do you like living alone on such a remote part of the property?"

"It's better than being at the main house. I love the land and working at Quinnland. Seemed like the best compromise."

She flashed her eyes at him. "Don't take this the wrong way. Is it because of your father? I mean, I've heard rumors that he isn't the easiest person to live with or be around."

"That's an understatement." He couldn't help but chuckle.

"Was it hard growing up with him?"

"I honestly don't remember. My brothers and cousins were always around. I guess having it tough with T.J. made us even closer. We looked out for each other, and I miss having them around. As far as T.J. goes, I pretty much make it a point to be where I know he isn't."

"How does that work out for you?"

"Fine. He doesn't get in my way and I don't get in his. We're two very different people who don't see eye-to-eye on much of anything."

She blew out a breath. "That's sad. You and your brothers have always been so kind to everyone." She flashed her eyes at him. "Don't get me wrong, everyone was clear if they messed with one Quinn the whole family stood behind him. It just seems like you guys grew up to be these great men and your father's missing out on it."

He hadn't thought of it in those terms. "I can't help but think we've missed out, too. When it comes to business and cattle ranching, the man is on top of his game. We could've learned a lot from him and Quinnland Ranch would be better off for it."

"I hear Isaac is back and I saw that he got married. Does your father have anything to do with the reason he's here?"

"T.J. has some big announcement he wants to make. He's asking everyone to come back to Quinnland so he can tell us all at once."

"Must be a pretty big deal if he wants everyone under one roof."

"There's no telling with T.J. He's well known for his bold moves. The man could've been a brilliant chess player. I have no idea what he plans to say." Not that his imagination hadn't run wild at times. Top of the list was that T.J. was terminally ill. Another was that his father planned to sell the ranch—Noah wouldn't put it past him, considering most of his siblings had moved away with no plans to come back.

"And he won't give you a hint?"

Noah shrugged his shoulders, like it rolled right off him. He could lose his mind trying to figure out T.J.'s machinations.

Mikayla studied him intensely for what felt like a solid minute. She took a bite of food and put her fork down. "You're hiding something."

"What makes you think so?"

"You care."

"The announcement could impact my life considering I live and work on the ranch. I'm concerned for any potential curveballs that might make my job harder."

"No. You care about him."

"You've lost your mind now."

"Have I?" She picked up her fork and took another bite of food.

Noah wanted to put up an argument. Nothing came to mind. Rather than spew empty words, which he was no good at anyway, he took a minute to think about what she said.

"T.J. has been making an effort lately.'" He could give her that much. "Can't say I'm optimistic just yet."

∽

"Maybe you'll find it in your heart to give him another chance." Mikayla wasn't flattering Noah a few minutes ago. The omelet was the best she'd had in longer than she could remember. Then there was the undeniable fact there was something incredibly sexy about a man who knew his way around the kitchen.

"Might be worth a try after I know what he's up to." He smiled at her with the kind of smile that literally weakened knees. It was laced with all that Quinn charm and devastating when aimed at her.

"What could it hurt?" As soon as the words came out she heard the irony in that statement. Her own heart immediately threw up a protest. Let herself fall for a man like Noah and it could end up shredded into a thousand tiny pieces.

And yet with him sitting there in her house, talking about things that mattered in his life, she knew she'd already strapped on for the roller coaster ride. Letting her guard down didn't come easy to Mikayla. She'd made a couple of bad choices when she wore her heart on her sleeve. The one before Bode, Zach Pozzier, had had a kid she'd opened her heart to. The breakup had nearly done her in. A few months later, she'd been given the news she wouldn't be able to have children of her own.

What had started as painful monthly cycles had ended up a years-long journey with laparoscopic surgery and a diagnosis of stage four endometriosis. She'd gone through four doctors before finally finding the one who could correctly diagnose her. The waiting, the not knowing what was wrong had been awful and probably the most stressful part. Not being able to talk to another person about what was going on had been hard. Her friends had moved away by then and it wasn't something she could just work into casual conversation on the rare times she got together with someone from her past.

She knew her body. She knew something wasn't right. She knew the minute she gauged a doctor's reaction to her complaints when she wasn't being taken seriously.

And then learning she might never have a family of her own had knocked the wind out of her.

Granted, she wasn't ready for marriage and family right this red-hot minute. But to never have the chance to be a mother? To have a family?

She couldn't go there.

Mikayla was getting choked up thinking about it. Time to move on to a different topic. Dwelling on the hand she'd been dealt wouldn't change a thing. It would only make her sad.

"Griff mentioned having someone come stay with you tonight. If you don't have any objections, I'd like to be that person. And before you answer, I fully expect to sleep on the couch."

"What about Callie? Will she be all right if you stay?"

"I can call and make arrangements for her to stay at the main house. Marianne jumps at the chance to spend time with her and she can sleep in the barn with Cody."

"Is that Brittany's Labrador?"

"Yes."

"I heard about him. How's he doing?"

"Better every day; he and Callie seem to have made fast friends. She's not used to sleeping in a barn but the place is hardly rustic. It's probably better insulated than our cabin."

"You could always bring her here." It might be nice to have a dog in the house. Mikayla had always wanted one and this might be the closest she'd get with her hectic schedule.

"We could do that. It would be easy enough to swing by the house and pick her up." Noah walked over to Mikayla and took the seat next to her. "Are you up for leaving the house?"

"I feel safe with you, Noah."

He smiled, which was a thousand tons of wattage coming at her all at once. He reached out and took her hand in his. "I'm sorry someone used my identity to hurt you. It must've felt like I was the one pushing you away when we were just getting to know each other."

"Do you think it's true? That someone is trying to punish me?" She visibly shivered.

"My first thought is that it's going to end up being someone who was close to you. From everything I've been taught about crimes against women, the perp is usually someone they knew and trusted." His jaw clenched. A man like Noah would take that fact personally. Call it Cowboy Code, or just plain being honorable, but any decent Texan would take issue with a woman being hurt by someone she knew. He added, "No man, woman or child should ever hurt anyone or anything smaller or weaker than they are."

The passion in his eyes when he spoke sent a firebolt to her heart. He was right. She absolutely believed the same thing. She'd also watched one of those true crime series on television that had echoed his sentiments about a woman's biggest threat being her husband or an acquaintance.

Her own father had died when she was too young to remember him. She'd grown up an only child with no male cousins to learn from. Mikayla hadn't grown up around men.

According to her mother, Mikayla's father had been a good person. Based on the stories she'd heard about him growing up, he seemed like the kind of person she would've loved to have been around.

Life had a way of taking things away from Mikayla before she had a chance to get used to them.

"Bode? Is that who you think is responsible?" Mikayla rubbed her wrists. She couldn't fathom anyone she knew doing something so horrific. But Bode was probably the only person who made sense when she thought about the crime in terms of someone she knew.

The Bowery boys were another possibility. And she couldn't rule out the Bridget sisters even though they'd only made catty remarks. Though in reality, they were like little yapping dogs; the darn things might make a lot of noise but there was nothing to back it up.

Mikayla bit back a yawn. Her full stomach after having a shower was most likely responsible for making her sleepy. Then again, she hadn't had much rest in the past twenty-four hours.

Exhaustion struck harder and faster than a physical blow.

Noah's brow went up when she yawned for the second time in a minute.

"I'm not ready to throw the book at anyone. I'd like to know where a few people were last night before I make any assumptions. See if a few key people can account for their whereabouts," Noah said.

"I should lie on the couch for a few minutes." She picked up her plate and deposited it into the sink.

She knew in her heart and it should be obvious to everyone involved that Noah had nothing to do with the crime, but it was his DNA that was going to show up everywhere.

Grateful for the comfortable blanket splayed over the back of the sofa, she pulled it over her as she curled up on her side.

"Mind if I close my eyes for a few minutes?"

He shook his head.

"Make yourself at home. Laptop is over there." She pointed to the glass coffee table. "You already know where the bathroom is. Help yourself to anything in the kitchen."

He walked over and picked up her laptop before glancing at her.

"There's no password since I never take it out of the house." She wondered how long Griff would be able to shelter his cousin if other law enforcement agencies got involved in the investigation.

A little voice in the back of her head said, *Not long.*

6

Mikayla sat up and rubbed her eyes as she woke from her nap. Exhaustion had caught up to her with the force of a freight train after breakfast, and even the cup of coffee she'd downed did nothing to combat it. "What time is it?"

"Four-thirty."

"I've been asleep six hours?" Noah was sitting at the table, same as when she'd closed her eyes. Though, she barely remembered doing it. She'd set him up with her laptop and told him to 'have at it.'

"Griff called. He said he'd meet us at the main house in half an hour." He stretched long, muscled arms and bit down a yawn. "Made sandwiches earlier. Think you can eat?"

"After I freshen up." She could get used to being spoiled like this. Being around a man who could take care of himself was a change; Bode's clingy nature and neediness had been the first two red flags he wasn't someone she would get along with long-term.

By the time she'd backtracked her way out of the relationship, his feelings had already become too strong, too fast. That had been the third and fatal red flag to having any kind of friendship.

Granted, she'd left things open-ended with him but that was mainly her way of easing away. She figured the distance from Gunner to San Antonio would do the rest for her. There'd been no big scene, which is why she couldn't fathom him coming back to abduct her.

She brushed her teeth, washed her face and then joined Noah at the table. He started to get up when she came in the room. "You don't have to, I can get a sandwich for myself. You already did the heavy lifting."

He smirked and damned if it wasn't sexy. "I'm not sure how heavy slapping meat, cheese, and lettuce in between two slices of bread is."

Mikayla shot him a look and then let herself laugh. "Fine. But you know what I mean."

"You have a beautiful smile, Mikayla. It's nice to see it."

Her cheeks flamed at the compliment. "Thank you."

The sandwich he'd described was nothing like the one wrapped up on a plate in her fridge. She eyeballed the layers, all of which he'd neglected to mention, including fresh-cut tomato and her personal favorite, mayonnaise. She poured a sparkling water and brought everything to the table, taking a seat next to him.

Being this close was probably a mistake because her breath quickened and her heart thundered in her chest. She was suddenly hyperaware of his all-male presence; his hands, his broad shoulders. His chiseled-from-granite features and those perfect, full lips.

Suddenly, all she could think about was the last kiss she'd shared with Noah. Since the best way to defeat a bear was to stare it in the face, she turned toward Noah, grabbed fistfuls of his shirt and tugged him toward her.

It didn't take much coaxing to get him to face her. The next thing she knew his thighs were on either side of hers. She dropped her hands to his as he brought his hand up to her chin. The flash of need in his eyes awakened places inside her that had been long-neglected.

He tilted her face toward his and brought his mouth down against hers. She closed her eyes and surrendered to the glorious tide sweeping over her and through her that was everything Noah. She breathed in his clean and spicy scent.

When his tongue darted inside her mouth, she let out a little moan that seemed to intensify the moment. He tasted like dark roast coffee, her favorite.

In the next second, she dropped her hands and squeezed solid thigh muscles. The heat in that moment struck her as the most she'd ever experienced with a man, any man, and especially from a kiss. She could only imagine what taking the next step with Noah would be like.

A slow ache coiled from her core, and then climbed, taking over every other sensation. All rational thought flew out of her mind as need overtook her. She had no doubt making love to Noah would be mind-blowing. Her body craved it more than she could fathom.

He pulled back enough to say, "You're beautiful." He moved his hand to the base of her neck, his thumb pad making little circles where her pulse pounded.

She nipped his bottom lip and felt his muscles cord underneath her fingers. The power she had to make his body react to her was heady. It also egged her on. As she brought her hands up to his shoulders, the sound of a cell phone buzzing interrupted the moment.

"Dammit," he said under his breath, his lips moving against hers as he spoke. "This had better fucking be important."

The sound of his frustration matched hers.

He turned to pick up his cell from the table. The screen indicated a text message from Griff.

On my way to the ranch now.

Noah slid the cell across the table, away from them, and turned back to her. "Where were we?" His voice was husky, gravelly and all kinds of sexy.

"I want this to happen, Noah." She tried to slow her breathing. She glanced at the rope burns on her wrists, torn between her longing for him and the niggling fear at the back of her mind about her abductor that she just couldn't shake. "But I need to know who did this to me."

"It's okay. I agree with you. We need to get going." He grunted and she couldn't agree more with his frustration. "And, Mikayla..."

She blinked up at him unable to catch enough of her breath to form coherent words.

"When we make love." He put careful emphasis on the word *when.* "You should know right up front that I have no plans to rush it. I intend to draw out every tingle in your body and make every single moment flush with pleasure for you."

A comment like that should put a fire in her cheeks. There was heat all right. And a hundred butterflies using her stomach as their personal playground.

"Ready?"

All she could manage was a smile and a nod. She stood and wrapped her sandwich up to take it with her before downing the sparkling water. Her hands were wobbly because she was so turned on she couldn't steady them. Her heart thundered in her chest and a *whoosh* sounded in her ears. Water sure tasted better than it did ten minutes ago.

"Give me a sec?" She took several slow, deep breaths as she tried to use her willpower to force her pulse to return to a normal rhythm.

Noah closed down her laptop and gathered up a few of his things while she threw on her usual outfit of a dress and her favorite boots. She ran a brush through her locks, resigned herself to them being untamed. She was good to go five minutes later.

In the living room, Noah waited at the door. Before she walked out, he stopped her and planted a tender kiss on her lips.

"I could get used to this," he said in that deep timbre that was so good at seducing her.

"I could, too." She couldn't afford to, but she offered a small smile.

In the truck on the way to the ranch, the sandwich tasted as good as it looked. It was gone by the time Noah pulled into the main entrance of his family's ranch. And it also gave her an excuse not to talk.

The problem was that she could very much get used to being with Noah. There was something down deep telling her that he was different, *this* was different than anything she'd ever experienced. And that selfish part wanted to let *this* play out despite all the reasons she had to nip it in the bud.

There was another part to her, the part that cared for other people more than she cared for herself, reminding her it wouldn't be fair to get into a relationship with man who was so clearly into family, when she couldn't give him one if things went well. It was probably putting the cart before the horse but what was the use starting down that path if it would only end in heartache?

"You've been doing some hard thinking on the way over here." He waved at the gate guard as if it were normal, like everyone grew up with one. "I hope you're not having regrets about what happened at your place, because that was the best kiss I've had in a long time."

How much should she tell him? They'd barely shared a few kisses and that didn't mean a trip down the aisle no matter how much her heart protested that this was different. They were just getting to know each other and God only knew if they'd want to see each other again, after all this was said and done. It was probably just the adrenaline, and the fact that he seemed to be the one person to make her feel safe after the nightmare of earlier. So, yeah, the whole idea of thinking about marriage and family now was definitely putting the cart before the horse.

"Same for me, Noah." She decided to table those thoughts for the time being. Because the selfish part of her wanted to spend a little more time with the man who'd awakened her in ways she had only heard or read about until now. "I'm just hoping you'll make good on your promise."

That brought on the wattage. Noah's smile could light the city of Austin in a blackout. "What can I say? I'm a man of my word."

He parked and then opened the door. She looked at the massive house with an impressive set of barns around the side. What must it have been like to grow up here?

Mikayla's childhood had been a happy one. She and her mother got along and Mikayla started working at the gas station after school and during her summers from an early age. She'd loved restocking shelves and working the register. A few of the nice deliverymen would bring her a sucker or a small stuffed toy they'd collected from one of their other stops from time to time. The house she grew up in had enough food and plenty of love. And she'd bought her own horse when she became old enough to take care of it by herself—that had been the deal.

What could she say? Some teenagers wanted cars for their sixteenth birthdays and others wanted horses. She happily fell into the second camp.

Considering she and her mother were together at the gas station all day and ate together most every night, she'd been fine to share a car.

Mikayla had a two-year degree from a community college a couple of towns over, which had taken her four years to complete part-time. But most of her friends had gotten married or moved away from Gunner for careers, and she could admit the past few years had felt a little lonely without them.

"Hold on." Noah dashed over to open her door for her even though she was already exiting the truck.

A man she recognized as Noah's brother Isaac came out the front door with an adorable little girl on his arm. Her strawberry-blonde hair on top of her head with a small bow made Mikayla's heart melt.

Isaac had never looked happier and that little girl's face beamed.

"Good to see you, Mikayla." Isaac didn't seem shocked she was there with Noah. He must've been informed of the situation. Of course, she thought, Noah worked on the ranch. He'd been missing today and that wouldn't go without an explanation. He wasn't the kind of person to leave his family hanging.

The brothers greeted each other with a bear hug, their closeness obvious. Seeing them almost made her wonder what it would've been like to grow up with a sibling. She'd relied on friends to have her back in high school. Clearly, she hadn't run in the same circles as the Bridget sisters. Somehow, even if she had, she doubted they'd be friends now.

The sound of tires on cement and gravel caught her attention. Griff's SUV came rolling up the drive.

"Let's go inside and talk."

Griff had that determined look he always got when he had news to report. Noah led the group into the house and the kitchen. He kept Mikayla's fingers linked with his. The Quinns could be a rowdy bunch, overwhelming to outsiders, and he wanted her to be comfortable with his family.

"Mikayla, I believe you already know my brother Isaac. Have you met Marianne?"

"I don't think we've met officially." Mikayla walked over and shook Marianne's hand. "I'm Mikayla."

"Wow. I haven't seen you since you were this tall." Marianne lowered her right hand to waist level. She smiled her approval, and then she shot a sly wink at Noah. "Make yourself at home."

Everyone took a seat around the kitchen table, except for Isaac. Marianne seemed to catch on. She took the baby from his arms, excused herself and disappeared down the hallway. Isaac took a seat across from Noah.

"We got ahold of Bode. He says that he worked like usual, met a few people from the office for drinks after work. Said he had one too many, caught a ride home from a friend and then crashed on the couch watching TV."

"Is it true?"

"The bartender where he had drinks at La Amiga remembers him coming in. Five people squeezed into a four-top table, had a round of appetizers and were served several drinks. One of the guys who fit Bode's description got loud and was asked to leave."

"He's not a big drinker." Mikayla seemed confused.

"Which could explain why he was drunk. He wasn't used to drinking and overestimated his ability to handle a few beers." Noah offered the explanation, but something felt off.

"From what I knew of him, he was a one and done guy. He didn't really like the taste of beer. I asked him why he drank at all if that was the case, and he said he only did when he went out with the guys.

Said he did it to fit in." The fact that Mikayla knew the man's habits shouldn't rub Noah the wrong way. He rolled his shoulders to ease the sudden tension.

"Did the person who gave him a ride home stay with him or drop him off?"

"Said they dropped him off around six-thirty. The witness gave the same story."

"Technically, he could've made it to Gunner in time." The bad feeling niggled a little more.

"If he'd been sober and somehow made it back to his vehicle," Griff acknowledged.

"He used to have a motorcycle. Said he was planning to sell it, so I'm not sure." It was Mikayla's turn to tense. She must not like talking about someone she'd dated with Noah in the room any more than he liked hearing about it.

It was important to discuss Bode. Personal feelings had to take a backseat to solving the case, so Noah put his in check.

"The bartender said Bode's vehicle remained at the bar at least through closing at two a.m. when his shift ended." Griff held up a hand. "Which doesn't mean he didn't grab a ride to get it and then take it back. It would be tricky. I'll have his license checked for C class and see if he has a registration for a motorcycle."

"My guess is that he does." Noah would put money on it.

"He's not the one I came to talk about this evening."

7

"Is there a better suspect than Bode?"

"What do you know about Miguel Cerano?" The coffee shop worker who brought Mikayla her favorite latte every Friday?

"Not much outside of the fact he starts making my order as soon as he sees me pull up in the parking lot."

"Did that ever strike you as odd?"

"I thought it was good customer service. He knew my name and I took it as another sign he'd been trained well to take care of his customers." She'd never thought of him as creepy so much as attentive.

"He called in sick yesterday and today." Griff's gaze shifted to Noah. "The coffee shop is on your list of the places you've been in the past two weeks. Is it possible you left your cell phone on the table or bathroom counter?"

"Anything's possible. Like I said before, I'm bad about keeping track of that thing since it's pretty useless out on the ranch. If it wasn't for Eli and Dakota, I wouldn't own one at all. It's always an afterthought and I seem to be forever looking for it when I need it."

Noah gently squeezed her hand. His fingers were linked with hers, their joined hands resting on her thigh.

"I sent a deputy to speak to Cerano at his house and he didn't answer."

"If he really was sick he might not have been up to answering the door," Mikayla offered.

"His manager caught him taking pictures of you when you weren't looking. He mentioned it didn't strike him as all that strange at the time. But when I asked if Cerano knew you, it was the first thing that popped into his thoughts."

"Seems like some people are notorious for taking low-key pictures and putting them on social media these days." Granted, she didn't like what she heard but it wasn't exactly criminal and didn't signal a fixation.

Noah issued another grunt. "One of many reasons I prefer working the land and minding my own business. I'd rather live my life than watch others."

Mikayla wouldn't argue there. She liked being able to stay in touch with friends who'd moved away through social media, but some people seemed to use the technology for more nefarious purposes.

"I checked Cerano's social media accounts and there aren't any pictures of you. He does have a lot of postings about being in love with someone and them not knowing or reciprocating. His manager thinks Cerano is talking about you." Griff fished his cell out of his pocket and pulled up one of the accounts. He set the cell on the table. "Can you look at the dates of the posts and determine whether or not you'd visited the coffee shop on any of those days?"

"Should be easy enough. I go there every Friday, as an end of the week treat, because I always run packages to the post office for the station." The time before last she'd run into Noah and his brother along with Isaac's new wife and adorable stepdaughter. That encounter had come after she'd received the another bad text from him. In retrospect, she'd acted like a jerk. "His posts are consistent. Once a week. Fridays."

Griff made a notation.

"Surely, I'm not the only customer who comes in on Fridays only."

"Probably not. It's just one of the angles we're following up on." Of course, he'd already mentioned Cerano's manager had said he had a crush on her. That part was creepy, but didn't mean he was a... what? A kidnapper? A murderer?

"You mentioned the attacker could've been around Noah's size."

"That's right. Cerano is smaller." But then most men were. "Honestly, I was caught by surprise, attacked, and even after coming to and having time to process everything, my memories are still a little blurry."

Isaac, who had been quiet up to now, chimed in. "The suggestion was already planted in your mind that you were meeting my brother. Is it possible the person who kidnapped you could have been significantly smaller and you wouldn't have realized?"

When she really thought about it, yes. "That's a good point. I expected it to be Noah, so my mind was set. I never got a good look at my attacker."

If she could go back to before the attack had happened and change one thing, it would be that she would've confronted Noah personally when she'd gotten the first text. The past twenty-four hours might've turned out a lot differently if she had.

Noah seemed to notice her getting inside her head when he said, "It's not your fault. You did nothing wrong."

There was something reassuring about hearing those words.

Griff was already nodding his head in agreement before his gaze shifted to his cousin. "Noah, I don't have to tell you this, but your DNA is all over two crime scenes."

"Stupidity on my part."

"Stupid is knowing what you're walking into and screwing up evidence. You're anything but. You had no idea what was going on and after finding Mikayla in the state she was in, no one blames you for rendering aid."

"I couldn't leave her like that until a deputy arrived. Plus, I had to get her out of the area. There was no telling when the jerk who'd done that to her would return or who he'd have with him when he did."

Griff nodded. "Getting her out of there considering you had no backup and no phone was an admirable decision." Griff paused like he was contemplating his next words carefully. "To an outside agency, and I hope it doesn't come to that, you would be on top of the suspect list. Which is why it's important for me to include you in every step of this investigation. An outsider might think you didn't buy a new cell phone because you knew exactly where yours was all along."

"But that's not true." Mikayla didn't doubt Noah's innocence for one second.

Noah squeezed her hand again for reassurance. "He's playing devil's advocate and I understand why. If I'd abducted her, it's not logical that I would've saved her and then brought her to the law. I'd have done whatever I'd set out to do to her."

"My argument exactly. I just want to prepare you for what might come your way. If another agency takes over the investigation, I'll have to be hands off. I have no doubt they'll reach the same conclusion."

"Understood." Noah leaned forward and placed his free arm on the table. "Did you have someone talk to the Bridget sisters?"

"I did. You remember their cousin, Derby. He's big enough to pull off something like this. He doesn't tie into your phone unless you left it somewhere he visits. We have to remember someone had access to you and your phone. That's key."

"How did they react to your visit?"

Mikayla tried not to act too interested in the response. She knew better than to let two shallow people's opinions hurt her feelings. Their words had stung because she believed them. Noah deserved to be with someone he could settle down with for the long haul. Being here at the ranch and seeing him interact with his family reminded her just how important having a family of his own would be to him.

A little voice in the back of her head also reminded her they were just getting to know each other. Sure, this felt different, and because of that she had no idea how it would play out. Her heart was already more attached than she knew better to allow.

The question wasn't if she liked Noah. The issue was, should she let whatever was happening between them go anywhere, when she knew being together long-term wasn't an option? Shutting it down before it grew legs might just be the kindest act for him. And for her own heart.

"Have you spoken to him?" Isaac's voice brought her out of her heavy thoughts.

"The interview is in progress now. Deputy Hernandez promised to send a text as soon as he's done."

Isaac sighed sharply. "I know these things take time but, damn. I don't like being on this side of the interview table with my brother."

It was easy to see the tight bond between brothers and there was something about their closeness that made her feel, for the first time in her life, that maybe she'd missed out on something in not being part of a big family. She imagined big Christmas parties, amazing food and laughter. Pretty much a full house with dogs barking, kids running around, exhausted parents and more happiness than any one person could handle.

This year, Mikayla and her mother had spent Christmas curled up on the sofa, watching a holiday movie and nibbling on snacks. Considering that it was just the two of them, and the gas station opened three-hundred-and-sixty-five days a year, they'd skipped having a traditional full-blown meal. Neither had had the time to shop or the energy to cook, but they'd baked brownies and grabbed a tub of vanilla ice cream.

The image of her mother in the kitchen helping bake brownies instead of being so tired from standing all day that she had to put her feet up brought on an unexpected wave of nostalgia. Her mother deserved lots of love and family surrounding her. Mikayla would never be able to give that to her.

Griff stood. "It doesn't sound like much but we're making progress. Try to get some rest tonight and hopefully we'll have more to go on by morning. I'm calling in all the favors I can think of in order to speed this investigation along. From every angle, it looks like this person is targeting Mikayla but that could be an illusion. No young woman is safe until we get this jerk behind bars as far as I'm concerned."

Isaac turned to Noah after Griff left the room. "We'll figure out who this bastard is and make sure justice is served."

Mikayla heard the hint of desperation mixed with a healthy dose of frustration in Isaac's tone.

∾

Noah appreciated everything Griff was doing to put the jerk who'd hurt Mikayla behind bars. It couldn't happen fast enough for Noah's liking.

Eli came through the back door, a baby in one arm and a toddler's hand in the other. Noah stood and retrieved a high chair and helped Eli put his son, Oliver, in it.

"You just missed Griff." Noah briefed his brother on what had gone down.

"I hear what he's saying about having to involve you but that part rankles." Olivia, his brother's four-month-old, sat happily blowing spit bubbles in his lap. Oliver, who was a few months more than a year, babbled in a language only he and Isaac's stepdaughter, Everly, seemed to understand. Those two had taken to each other from day one.

Noah couldn't help but notice how happy Isaac was recently. His thoughts shifted to Mikayla and he couldn't help but wonder what it would be like to have a family with her.

Even though it had only been a few days, his brother Isaac and his new family had seemed like they'd been part of the group forever.

Gina, Isaac's new bride, had fit in from the start and a large part of the reason probably had to do with the fact that she'd grown up in Gunner and had a history with Isaac. Neither had truly ever stopped loving the other even though he'd gone into the military as soon as he'd turned eighteen and she'd moved to Dallas.

Eli had had a whirlwind relationship with a Fort Worth socialite. The two had seemed into each other and Eli was, as far as Noah could tell, head over heels for his wife, Camille.

Camille, on the other hand, seemed to have romanticized ranch life. Once she got a taste for what life on a ranch really was, she'd bolted and given custody of the kids to Eli.

His oldest brother was an amazing father and had pulled a short straw when it came to picking the right woman to share his life with. Camille didn't look back once after Olivia was born. Divorce papers had shown up within twenty-four hours of her moving back to Fort Worth. She must've been planning this for most of her pregnancy.

"Any word on hiring a babysitter for the kiddos?" Noah needed to change the subject away from discussing the case. He could tell it was wearing thin on Mikayla and overthinking it wouldn't do any good. He'd found a long time ago when he had a problem that needed solving the best thing he could do was think about something totally unrelated. It always amazed him how much faster answers came when he wasn't hunting for them.

"Haven't found the right person yet." Noah figured a piece of his brother wasn't ready to accept that Camille had moved on. Granted, she'd hurt him like hell.

Mikayla folded her arms like she was shoring up her strength as she looked at the babies. A mix of emotion passed behind her eyes. Sadness? Regret? And then she smiled at them. Was that wistfulness that he saw in her eyes?

"How long before dinner?" Noah asked.

Isaac checked his watch. "Half hour or so."

Good. That would give him enough time to show Mikayla the grounds. She'd been resting, he'd been sitting most of the day, and he figured both of them could stand to stretch their legs. He tugged at her hand and felt like a teenager when he asked, "Want to check something out?"

Her eyes lit up and he could feel the energy radiating from her as she nodded.

"We'll be back in a bit." The others waved them on.

Noah wanted to show her the barns and he needed to check on Callie. And then there was the black Labrador. He'd made a home in the barn after Brittany, his owner, had been murdered and Cody had been injured. He'd been in bad shape when friend and vet, Michael, had first treated him. Slowly, he was improving.

Cody missed his owner and keeping him happy would go a long way toward his healing. Noah had seen it time and time again with animals on the ranch. A positive spirit was so much a part of healing. A broken one sent an animal into a spiral that rarely turned out the way Noah would like. He figured people could be the same.

Outside the house, he felt a tug on his hand. He turned toward Mikayla, who was already bringing her other hand up to his shoulder. She released his hand and brought the other one up to rest on his other.

She pushed up on her tiptoes and planted a kiss full of promise on his lips. "I've needed to do that for the past hour."

A thunderclap of need struck Noah. He didn't want to think about how much having her in his arms, his lips pressed to hers, soothed places inside him that had been dark too long.

8

"She's been by his side most of the day." Noah turned to see Dakota leaning against the office door; he must have heard them come inside the barn.

"She probably heard the truck earlier and realized I'd be home." Noah bent down to scratch Callie in her favorite spot.

"Name's Dakota Viera." He held out his hand toward Mikayla.

She took the offering. "Mikayla Rae Johnson."

"I believe I've seen you before, but I can't for the life of me place where."

"My mom and I own the gas station near the highway."

"Ah. Right. I don't go inside much but I've been through there quite a bit. Nice to officially meet you."

"You, too. Stop inside next time you're at the pump and say hello. We love getting to know our customers." With her beauty and easy way with people, Noah figured plenty of folks took her up on the offer. A stab of jealousy struck and it almost made him chuckle. He was doing one helluva job keeping his emotions in check when it came to Mikayla.

The black lab's tail was going a mile a minute.

"Hey there, Cody." Noah eased toward the eager boy as Callie came around, placing herself in between him and the other dog. "She's either jealous that I'm talking to another dog or protecting him from potential danger."

"Maybe a little of both." Dakota stood just over the six-foot mark, arms now folded over his chest. "She knows you wouldn't hurt him but instinct takes over at some point and she must realize the shape he's in."

"It's only been a couple of weeks. I'm impressed with his progress so far."

Mikayla sat down next to Cody. "I heard about him from one of our customers. He survived despite impossible odds. Would he let me pet him?"

Noah nodded. Her compassion hit him square in the chest.

"Should I be careful of any areas?"

"Avoid his chest. He was severely cut. Fortunately for him, Gina came along when she did." The timing was not so lucky for his new sister-in-law because while she called for help for Cody, the killer sneaked up on her from behind and knocked her out.

Not unlike what had happened to Mikayla when he really thought about it. A copycat? The man responsible for Brittany's death was locked behind bars with an iron-clad confession to ensure justice was served for her murder. Bo Stanley wouldn't hurt another woman for the rest of his days.

What he'd done to Brittany might've given someone else an idea, though.

"I'm sorry for what you're going through. I hope you don't mind but Isaac gave me a heads-up when Noah didn't return from the feed store this morning. If there's anything I can do to help, you let me know."

"That's a kind offer, Dakota. Right now, I think we're just trying to figure out who and why." Mikayla's genuine smile would warm Alaska in winter.

"The why might help us figure out the who," Noah interjected.

"Thought I saw Griff's SUV at the house."

"He just left."

"Did he mention admirers? If you don't mind my saying, a pretty woman like you might have a few." Dakota voiced Noah's fear. The attacker had used the situation to lure her out and had left no trail leading back to him. There were the obvious suspects, but Dakota made a point in that it could literally be any strong male in and around Gunner who'd come across Noah's phone. He never used the password protect feature because he didn't put anything important in there. That was something he'd definitely rectify going forward.

Mikayla shrugged. Her cheeks flushed from the compliment. It was beyond crazy to Noah that she had no idea how beautiful she was inside and out. Her warmth and kindness only added to her physical beauty. Face it, outward good looks only got a person so far in his book. Getting to know a shallow person took all of one date, and not a good one at that.

Real beauty came from the light inside a person, and Mikayla was the real deal. Part of him wanted T.J. to meet her, which was odd considering he'd never needed his father's approval and still didn't.

"Have you seen T.J. around today?" Noah's father didn't believe in keeping an office aside from the one in the main house, so he only showed for morning meetings.

Dakota shook his head. "I'm assuming you mean other than this morning."

Would T.J. show at supper? Since Noah didn't usually do family dinner nights, he had no way of knowing.

"What about Jess?" Noah had blown off the greenhorn this morning and guilt nipped at him for not being more patient with the young guy.

"Not lately. He's probably still out checking fences. He must've asked if you were okay half a dozen times this morning."

"Me?"

Dakota shrugged. "What can I say? You seem to have reached superhero status with the kid. You're his idol. I would caution you to be careful. Seems a little fragile on the emotions."

"What makes you say that?"

"He took it a little hard when you took off without saying hello this morning." Dakota threw his hands in the air. "I know. It's a bit much. But he's still a kid and he's been through a lot in his short life."

"He still not talking about what he saw?"

"Not to me. We've helped some rough cases before." Dakota slapped his chest. "Me included, but this one feels different. We're all looking out for this kid and hoping for the best."

"I'll square things up with him." Noah really hadn't intended to hurt the kid's feelings.

"Just be ready for a shadow because this kid thinks you hang the moon." Dakota had a point there.

Jess had a juvenile record that was sealed. He wasn't talking, so they had no idea what they were actually dealing with and all they knew for certain was the kid had experienced a trauma that had driven him to commit a crime. Before that, he'd been in and out of the foster system. He'd been released at eighteen-years-old without any family to take care of him, in and out of trouble, moving from ranch to ranch amassing an unsteady work record. Quinnland was most likely the kid's last hope. If he couldn't find himself here, there might not be another place for him.

Noah had trouble accepting defeat and had a soft spot for anyone or thing in trouble. He'd brought every wounded animal he came across into the barn to nurse back to health. Over the years, a few seasonal ranch hires had said it would be his downfall. He hoped not. Compassion wasn't a sign of weakness in his book.

"You keep healing and you'll be up and around in no time," he whispered to Cody. The lab had a spark in his eyes and he seemed to have taken an equal shine to Callie. "I'll check on the greenhorn later. Marianne will be calling for supper soon. Are you coming?"

"Not me. I already have lasagna in the office fridge and more paperwork than I know what to do with."

"This may not have been the best time to bring on another greenhorn," Noah joked.

"That's a little too real to be funny."

"Oh, that reminds me. Before you take off, your buddy left something for you. Hold on here. Let me find it." Dakota moved to his desk that was pushed up against the north-facing wall. He rummaged around on top, shifting paperwork around. "Where'd I put that thing?" He opened and closed a couple of drawers.

After moving a few more stacks of papers, Dakota said, "A-ha. Knew I'd find it." He moved to Noah and handed over his favorite horse brush.

"I wondered what happened to this." Noah held up the wood and bristle brush.

"The darn thing turned up today. Jess had it, said he found it in Red's stall."

"Guess there's some advantage to having a shadow." Noah laughed as he took the offering and then returned it to the tack room. "I'll be sure to thank him later." He squeezed Mikayla's hand. "Hungry?"

"Surprisingly, yes."

"I want to show you something before we head back to the main house."

Mikayla said goodbye to Dakota and reminded him to stop inside the gas station on his next visit.

Noah locked gazes with Mikayla. "You ready for a tour?"

∾

Quinnland was probably the most impressive place Mikayla had ever been privileged to see. The main house in and of itself would be considered massive by anyone's standards. The grounds? The lawn seemed to go on forever around the main house, a building apparently known as Casa Grande, and with good reason. Grande was actually a good word to describe pretty much everything at Quinnland, from the barn, to the house, to the acres of land all across the property itself.

The barn they'd just left had been remarkable. Stalls lined one side of the main area and offices sat across from them. The stalls gave the horses plenty of room to move around. They were clean. There was an area off to one side for washing the horses. The tack room was bigger than most living rooms. Tack was neatly organized and each horse had his or her labeled preferences.

Behind the barn was an impressive exercise ring. Again, it made the one where she boarded her horse look like child's play. But then the Quinns were a successful ranching family. Mikayla almost laughed out loud. Saying the Quinns were successful at ranching was like saying Colonel Sanders fried a little bit of chicken in his lifetime.

Noah walked with her along the tree line where hundreds of mesquites and oaks created a thicket in a crescent-shape around the back of the barn.

"What do you think?" Noah asked as he walked with her toward the main house.

"This whole place is a lot to take in. The barn…let's just say I feel bad for my mare after being inside your place."

"Do you ride every day?"

"No. And not nearly as much as I'd like to."

"You should think about keeping her here." He seemed to catch himself mid-sentence. Keeping her mare at his barn might be more than either were ready for. "All I mean is she'd have plenty of company, and if you couldn't get out to exercise her there's always someone here who could do it for you."

"It's something to think about." Prissy, her Arabian, would be in heaven on Quinn property. The stable she boarded at now wasn't horrible by any means, but it wasn't in this league. It was what Mikayla could afford. For Prissy's sake, Mikayla would consider taking Noah up on his offer. If she paid like everyone else it might not feel like charity. "Can I ask how much you'd charge a month?"

He made a face like he'd just sucked on a lemon and shook his head. "Nothing. We have extra room and it would give us a chance to see each other more if you rode here."

Noah turned toward her. She took a couple of steps back until she stood against the wall and smiled shyly up at him. Palms flat, he put a hand on either side of her and then he dipped his head down and kissed her. Two fists full of his shirt helped her pull his firm body against hers, where she melted.

He pulled back just enough to press his forehead against hers. "The stall next to my horse, Dusty, is vacant. Who knows, the two of them might just get along."

"Crazier things have happened." Of course, she couldn't make a major move for her horse on a whim. It would take careful consideration. If it worked out, Prissy would love this place, and it was easy to see she'd be well cared for while Mikayla was at work. "And that would mean we would be seeing a lot more of each other."

"Not really. I almost never go in the barn." His serious expression almost got her. Until he broke into a wide smile. "The barn would be a whole lot prettier if you were in it."

She looped her arms around his neck. "That so?"

"Uh-huh." He grazed her bottom lip with his tongue. Now she understood what it truly meant for someone to go weak at the knees.

"You're not so bad yourself." She captured his in her teeth.

Dropping his hands to her waist, he said, "Keep that up and we won't make it to dinner."

"We should probably eat."

"Yeah, but that would require moving and I kind of like it right where I am." Noah smiled, turning on his serious bright whites. The man was gorgeous. This close her stomach engaged in a freefall.

A noise sounded to Mikayla's left. The hairs on the back of her neck pricked. She had the feeling of being watched. She tracked the sound and dropped her hands immediately to her sides. Noah caught on and checked out what had her attention.

A young male around six-feet tall stood twenty feet away, frozen, staring at them.

"Hey, Jess. I've been meaning to come talk to you. Thanks for finding Dusty's brush."

The guy mumbled an apology before heading in the opposite direction.

Noah looked torn between chasing after him and leaving her alone at the barn.

"Should you go find him?"

He blew out a sharp breath. "Nah. I don't know what his problem is. I'll text Dakota when we get back to the main house and ask him to check on the kid."

Mikayla tried to shake off the creepy-crawly feeling. She almost pointed out that Jess wasn't a kid.

Noah linked their fingers and she held onto his forearm with her other hand. He pulled her in closer and wrapped his arm around her instead, letting the comfort that was Noah guide her toward the main house and away from those heavier thoughts.

Back inside, the family was assembling in the kitchen. She met Noah's newly minted sister-in-law, Gina. She'd heard a running joke that the Quinn family made up half the male population of Gunner. Noah had six brothers, two of whom were twins; then there were the cousins, the other Quinn brothers, who numbered five. In total, the male population of Quinn's under the age of thirty-five was a full dozen. She'd heard the running joke about the Quinn's making one helluva calendar.

As she watched Noah, Isaac, and Eli standing in the kitchen together, it was easy to see why folks believed the Quinn brothers and cousins would make a calendar that rivaled any hot firefighters'. Noah, in her humble opinion, would definitely be August. The hottest month in Texas needed the sexiest Quinn. He walked over to her where she stood next to the butcher block table.

"What's the smile all about?"

She shook her head. No way in hell was she planning to tell him that she'd been thinking about how hot him and his brothers were. She wasn't tripping into that pothole. To distract him from the fact she had no plans to answer his question, she kissed him.

He looped his arms around her and leaned his hip against the table. All those butterflies woke up and flitted around in her stomach. She'd thought it before, almost said it out loud, but she was in deep trouble with Noah Quinn. Not because he was beautiful to look at and made her think unholy thoughts. But because he was intelligent, and could make her laugh. He was honest and humble and earthy in the best possible way.

Someone made a throat-clearing noise. Mikayla pulled back from Noah and turned toward the sink to hide the fact her cheeks flamed.

Through the kitchen window, she saw the oldest Quinn in the backyard, his hand on the shoulder of the young man she'd seen a few minutes ago. Jess seemed upset and from what she could tell, T.J. looked to be comforting him. It went against everything she'd heard about the Quinn patriarch. The image of him consoling an upset ranch hand made her think he'd maybe turned a corner in his life. He was getting to an age where people reflected on their lives; she'd seen the same with her own mother.

It would be nice if her mother would get out more instead of staying home every night content to eat dinner alone while watching TV. When Mikayla really thought about it, she wasn't much better. Sure, she got out on the weekends on the occasional date. And she rode her horse every afternoon that she could after work.

But really living?

Going out with Noah had been the first time in a long time she'd seen herself being able to relax with someone. *Be* with someone. Conversation had been easy and interesting. They'd only dated a few times so she'd been surprised at how deeply she'd been hurt when the text had come.

T.J. pointed toward the barn, patted Jess on the back, and then turned toward the main house. She was about the meet the infamous T.J. Quinn, the man whose name put shadows in Noah's eyes.

9

"This kitchen smells amazing."

"Marianne deserves all the credit." Knowing Mikayla was happy in Noah's family home felt right. Like a fresh rain after a long draught.

Isaac and Eli were in deep conversation at the table, no doubt figuring out the answers to world peace. Oliver and Everly, similar in age, were in side-by-side high chairs babbling in more of that adorable baby speak only the two of them seemed to understand. Olivia was in Gina's arms. Gina beamed down at the little girl.

Noah thought he heard the porch door open and definitely saw Marianne slink that way from out of the corner of his eye. She seemed to be making great effort to go unnoticed so he didn't follow her or call her out.

"Do you mind finding seats for us at the table while I get drinks?"

Mikayla nodded and smiled. He liked that she felt comfortable enough to walk over and take a seat next to one of his brothers or new sister-in-law.

At the fridge, Noah heard whispers coming from the porch. He recognized the voices as T.J. and Marianne. Those two sounded awfully conspiratorial. But then, he didn't normally come to supper.

The last time Noah had sat down at the table with his father...hell, he couldn't remember when that was. He'd slept since then.

The fact T.J. and Marianne got along so well struck Noah as odd. They certainly didn't during his childhood. His father had been smart enough to realize she was the glue that had held this family together. If he and his brothers had turned out to be halfway decent men, it had been because of Marianne.

For all his faults, T.J. seemed to know when to leave things alone when it came to his sons. And, for the most part, his hiring skills had been flawless.

Conversation in the kitchen flowed even when T.J. walked into the room. Noah went back to pouring drinks, pretending not to have questions about what had just transpired on the porch. Maybe he should start spending more time in the main house if he wanted to know what was going on. He'd been content to live on the property and work the cattle. His view of the family home had been limited to what he could see from the barn.

Now that the Quinn kids had grown into men, Marianne probably worked closer with T.J. in order to keep busy. Granted, she'd been busy lately pinch-hitting for Eli, taking care of his kiddos while he worked.

Marianne walked to the sink, next to him. In the buzz of conversation, he figured he could slip in a question without drawing much attention.

"How'd the last babysitter interview go?" He nodded toward Eli.

Marianne shook her head. "She wasn't the right fit."

"Why not this time?"

"She didn't have a background in music."

"Music? What does that have to do with taking care of two little kiddos?"

She shrugged.

"I know you don't mind helping Eli out with the kids, but this is the busiest time on the ranch and I can tell he isn't getting much sleep. Why do you think he's dragging his heels on hiring help?"

"He doesn't want someone moving into his home to change

diapers and handle feedings or drop the kids off at daycare when they're old enough." Marianne looked out the window. A wistful expression overtook her smile. "You want my honest opinion?"

"Of course."

"He's trying to replace a mother. He wants to give them something they can't get from a stranger who is taking care of them for a paycheck. He wants someone who'll love them."

"When you put it like that I understand." He totally understood. Marianne had been that person for them when their mother had died after Phoenix was born.

"It's why I'm not in a hurry for him to hire. I don't mind the extra work and I'm one of the few people he trusts to love on those babies."

"You did a damn fine job raising us. Have I told you lately how much I appreciate everything you did and are still doing for my brothers and me?"

Noah could've sworn he saw moisture gathering in her eyes.

"Taking care of the seven of you has been one of the great privileges of my life." She sniffed and then covered by snapping, "It's also where all this gray hair came from."

"I'm pretty sure half of those came from me alone."

She laughed.

He picked up the drinks from the counter and as he turned, the expression on Mikayla's face speeded up his steps toward her.

"What's wrong?" He took the seat next to her and set the glasses down in front of them.

She stared at her cell phone screen, her face sheet-white.

"It's from Bode. He's here in Gunner. He wants me to meet him."

"Where in Gunner?"

"On his way to my mother's house."

Noah felt his temper rise. "He doesn't need to be in contact with you."

"I'm probably overreacting here but I don't like it." She had a point.

"I hear what you're saying. Logically, he'd be stupid to do anything to your mother while suspicion is on him." He tapped his index finger on the table. "If he's desperate and doesn't think he has anything to lose he could make an idiot move."

"She needs to be warned. If she knows not to open the door for him, she won't." Mikayla excused herself from the table and Noah followed her outside so she could make the call in private.

Her mother picked up on the first ring. "Mom, you're on speaker. I'm here with Noah."

"Hello, dear. Hi, Noah."

Before he could respond, Mikayla cut in, "Mom, I need you to do something for me. If anyone comes to the door, don't open it. Not even someone you think you know. Can you do that?"

"It's too late for that, honey. Your friend Bode Harding stopped by. He's here right now and he wants to speak to you. Hold on. I'll put him on the phone."

"Mikayla, we need to talk." Bode's voice had that hint of desperation Noah had been worried about.

"Fine. Meet me at the station. I can be there in less than half an hour."

"No. I'd rather meet here with family."

Noah could almost see the wheels turning in Mikayla's brain. He shook his head and kept quiet.

"And, Mikayla, don't bring anyone. I want to talk to you alone."

"Not a chance." Her mother had already given away the fact that she was with Noah, so there was no point trying to hide the fact now.

"What I need to say to Mikayla doesn't concern you, Noah."

"Like hell it doesn't."

There was a moment of silence between them Bode didn't seem ready to challenge. Then came, "I didn't do it."

Noah issued a grunt. The words *like hell* came to mind. He clamped his mouth shut. Poking the bear wouldn't get the answers he needed.

"I want to believe that's true, Bode." Noah paused a beat. "Here's the thing. Until the jerk is safely locked, I suspect every male in Texas could be guilty. You included. Until the truth is revealed and that bastard is behind bars, I'm taking no chances with Mikayla's safety. Whatever you have to say to her can be said over the phone."

"Not possible. Anyone could be listening." He was paranoid?

"Are you in trouble?"

A pregnant pause answered the question for Noah.

"My cousin is going to want to know about the fact you're reaching out to Mikayla."

"Don't tell anyone. This conversation can't get out." Bode was being sincere or he was one hell of an actor. The fear in his voice seemed genuine. Noah didn't know the man well enough to decide which way to lean. He could only go on instinct and experience having grown up with six siblings and five cousins had taught him a thing to two about how the male mind worked.

Bode was either at Mikayla's mother's house to scare Mikayla into doing what he wanted or because he was afraid to be seen in a public place and thought they'd have more privacy there. He'd probably tried Mikayla's house already and figured out she wasn't home.

The fact that Mikayla had phoned her mother meant his cell couldn't be traced back to this conversation. He most likely would've asked Mikayla's mother to call her.

If she agreed to meet him at her mother's house and he kidnapped her, logic said he'd get caught. Her mother was a witness, unless he planned to kill her to silence her. And what about now? He'd requested to speak to Mikayla alone knowing full well that Noah was aware of the conversation.

"Have you thought this through, Bode? Nothing good can come of this unless you leave Gunner, go home and let the investigation play out," Noah warned.

"I can't do that." Strange of him to admit if he was planning a double murder.

"Why not?"

His voice was muffled when he said, "Mrs. Johnson, could I have that glass of water now?"

MIKAYLA LOCKED GAZES WITH NOAH. Her lungs seized. Fear gripped her. Noah's steady gaze and calm demeanor kept her nerves a notch below panic.

"Here's the thing." Bode's voice wasn't much more than a whisper. "I wouldn't hurt Mikayla."

"You're going to have to do better than that, Bode."

"Mikayla, you remember that motorcycle I had?"

"Yes."

"I still have it and I used it last night." His normally calm-to-the-point-of-boring voice was erratic, like a heartbeat monitor on a patient who was crashing.

Mikayla bit back the urge to respond. The sound of her own heart jabbing her ribs filled her ears.

"That's all I can say on a cell. But there's so much more. No matter what happens, I need you to know I would never do anything to hurt you. I still care about you."

Noah white-knuckled the phone. Anger? Jealousy? To his credit, he kept silent even though she could almost see the words forming on his lips.

"Leave my mother out of this, Bode."

A voice sounded in the background. "Here you go." It was her mother's. No doubt returning with the glass of water he'd requested a minute ago.

"Thank you, Mrs. Johnson." His voice became loud and clear when he said, "I have to go, but I appreciate your hospitality."

Background noise came over the line and then her mother's blissful voice said, "Can I call you right back?"

Noah shook his head and clenched his jaw.

"No. Mom. I know this is going to sound like a strange request but keep me on the line. You can set the phone down to see Bode out, but I need to speak to you. Okay?"

"Oh, all right." Her mother sounded confused. At least she'd listened.

Then there were two voices in the background, too far from the receiver for Mikayla to make out what was being said. She could've sworn she heard a door close. The breath she'd been holding came out in a slow sigh when her mother's voice came back on the line.

"What did you want to speak to me about, honey?"

"Is Bode gone?"

"Yes."

"Can you move to the front window and check that he's pulling away?"

"I can hear his car, but I'll go check if it's important to you."

"It is, Mom." She needed to come up with a quick explanation to ward off the many questions that had to be building in her mother's mind. "After the ordeal last night, I'm overly paranoid."

"Bode's a decent person..." Her mother gasped. She seemed to catch on to the implication when she said, "He didn't...did he?"

"His name came up in the investigation. I don't want to scare you but don't trust anyone until we get this sorted out. Okay, Mom? Not even people you think you know and especially not anyone I know."

"Oh, honey. I hadn't thought this nightmare could get worse. But, yes, I see his car pulling out of the drive. He's on the street now. Should I call the sheriff?"

"No. It's okay. We can't let our guard down until the person who did this is behind bars." She didn't want to alarm her mother, so she didn't ask if he'd sounded threatening. And she didn't believe he had since he'd left without being forced.

Noah motioned toward his temporary phone.

"We'll call Griff and ask what he thinks about the visit. Stay inside until I get back to you and don't answer the door. Okay, Mom?"

"Does that mean the man who hurt you could come back?" Mikayla hated how shaky her mother's voice had become.

"He could. Griff is doing his job and working the investigation as fast and thoroughly as he can. Noah has promised to stay with me to see this through. I have as much protection as I can get without being locked in a vault."

"You're worried about him doing something to me?"

"I don't know what the jerk wanted with me in the first place and I have no idea how far he'll go to hurt me. The chances anyone would come to you are slim to none but I'm not risking your safety. I love you too much to let anything happen to you." In that moment, it dawned on Mikayla how alone she would be if anything happened to her mother. It had been the two of them for most of her life and she had no memories of a time when it wasn't just the pair of them. They'd become even closer as a result.

Noah motioned for her to put the phone away from her ear for a second. He whispered, "Think she'd come stay at the ranch for a while?"

"I can ask." Mikayla relayed the message.

Her mother's answer was as expected. "I don't want to put anyone out."

"Tell her I'll send a car to pick her up. You'll text when the driver is out front," Noah said.

Mikayla did.

"Only if it won't be any trouble."

Noah was already shaking his head.

"You could never be a bother, Mom."

"In that case, I'll pack a bag." Mikayla heard the eagerness in her mother's voice and a stab of guilt nailed her. Had she been neglecting her mother? She seemed awfully willing to hop in a car and be with people. It hadn't taken much to convince her to drop everything and stay at Quinnland.

"I'll see you in a little while. Love you, Mom." Mikayla didn't say it often enough but she felt those words every day.

"Love you, honey."

As soon as she ended the call, Noah had Griff on speaker. "Bode is in town and he admitted to owning a motorcycle."

"How do you know?"

"He just paid Mikayla's mother a visit. My guess is he stopped by Mikayla's house first. When she didn't answer, he went to her mom's place. He must've figured she'd be there after what she'd been through."

Griff muttered a few choice words under his breath and they were the same ones Mikayla was thinking.

"Here's the thing; he asked to speak to Mikayla alone when we called."

"So you spoke to him, but the call would look like it was between Mikayla and her mother?"

"That's right. Not exactly the actions of an innocent man, if you ask me."

"My thoughts exactly."

10

"Bill Bowery's boy hasn't been home since spring break. He was holed up in a study room most of last night working on a Lit paper due at nine o'clock this morning. His professor confirmed Bowery was in class." *Scratch one name off the list*, Noah thought.

"That's a solid alibi."

"He was always a wild card." Noah figured as much.

"I'll put out a Be On The Lookout for Bode. It's time for a face-to-face interview with Bode Harding."

"I have his cell number if you'd like to give him a call and ask him to come in voluntarily." Mikayla scrolled through her contacts, stopping on Bode's.

"Even better."

She rattled off the numbers to Griff.

"One of my deputies will get right on this."

"What about Miguel Cerano? Have you been able to catch up to him?" Noah figured he and Mikayla could pay the coffee shop a visit tomorrow morning and gauge Cerano's reaction to seeing her.

"Not yet." Griff agreed to keep them posted before ending the call. Noah figured this might be a good chance for him to show the greenhorn, Jess, that he had confidence in him. He called Dakota, who picked up on the first ring.

"I need a personal favor," Noah began.

"Name it." Dakota's loyalty, dedication, and willingness to go the extra mile were the attributes that moved him to the foreman position soon after he came to work at the ranch.

"Send the greenhorn to pick up Mikayla's mother and bring her back to the ranch." Noah added, "Tell him it's an important assignment and that I personally requested him for the job."

"That'll mean the world to him." Dakota paused a beat before adding, "He's not making the progress I'd hoped. I spoke to T.J. about him and he wants to give Jess a little more time to get straightened out. I caught him pocketing a few dollars from the petty cash drawer red-handed and he refused to admit it."

"Not a good sign for his future." A stab of guilt nailed Noah. If he worked with him a little more there was a chance he could be a better influence.

"No. It sure isn't. I'm hoping the best for him. Every kid deserves a chance to straighten his life out." The mantra had been T.J.'s. The man believed hard work would cure just about anything. Noah could admit the logic had some merit.

"Think he can be trusted with Mikayla's mother?"

Dakota issued a sigh. "As best as I can tell, yes. Your confidence might go a long way toward helping him open up. As it stands, he's on the road out of here."

"You can lead a horse to water..."

No one liked the idea of losing one. They'd known they were taking on a tough case with Jess. The sting of being so close to losing him was just as sharp. Noah had learned a long time ago that the best he could do was show the way in his own actions and show the other person he cared what happened. The rest was up to them.

"I know. I know." Dakota issued another sharp sigh. "Let's see if we can get this one to drink."

Noah ended the call. "We can stay here or at your place tonight. It's your call."

"Do you think Callie will be more comfortable at your house?"

"After seeing her with Cody earlier, my guess is she'll want to stay by his side." Noah linked his fingers with Mikayla's.

"I'd like to see your home."

"A tour won't take long." He extended his arms as far as he could stretch them. "It's about this big."

His joke netted a smile and an unexpected peck on the lips.

"I want to see where you live."

He brought his mouth down onto hers and thoroughly kissed her. When he pulled back they were both a little breathless. "Then, we're going to my place later. But first, are you hungry?"

"How could I not be? The smell of food a little while ago practically made my stomach growl."

Noah led them back to the kitchen. Food was already on the table. Folks were chatting easily as they dined. Even T.J. was in the mix along with Marianne, who seemed to sense his discomfort. She sat beside him and engaged in conversation with Gina.

Marianne and T.J.'s whispering earlier on the porch came to mind. It wouldn't surprise Noah if she knew something about the big announcement, though he had his doubts as to whether or not a couple of his brothers would come home for it.

After losing their mother, T.J.'s heavy-handedness had driven some of Noah's brothers away, with promises they'd never set foot on the property again.

T.J. might have to compromise and set up a phone conference. Noah suppressed the laugh threatening to break free from his chest. The words *compromise* and *T.J.* didn't belong in the same sentence.

Liam, Isaac's twin, might never set foot at Quinnland after the argument he'd had with their father a handful of years ago. T.J. had been his usual stubborn self, refusing to listen to reason. After Liam's young and pregnant wife had been in a horrific freak accident involving a tractor, T.J. had told his son to *Buck up and move on.* Their father had been as comforting as snuggling a porcupine.

T.J. didn't tolerate emotions he didn't understand. He and Liam had gotten into one helluva dust-up the following Christmas. Liam hadn't been home in seven years. He'd visited Gunner to see his brothers and niece and nephew, but kept to his word about never setting foot on T.J.'s property again.

Casa Grande should feel strange to Noah. Being back in the main house should feel off. Surprisingly, it didn't and he knew without a doubt the woman seated next to him made all the difference.

Halfway through the meal, Mrs. Johnson was led into the room by Dakota. Her eyes lit up the minute they landed on her daughter. The men at the table stood and welcomed her, each introducing himself. Gina followed suit before Mikayla embraced her mother.

There was a faint resemblance between mother and daughter, noticeable mostly when they smiled. Mrs. Johnson had a full head of gray hair in a short, spikey cut that added to her spunky personality. At no more than five-feet-two-inches tall, she had a kind face and enough wrinkles to show she laughed often. He already knew she was dedicated to the gas station she and her daughter owned and ran as a team. Clearly a hardworking, salt-of-the earth type. The kind he wouldn't be a bit surprised if she had a small vegetable garden in her backyard.

"Please, sit with Marianne and me." T.J.'s offer was met with a warm smile.

Noah had to practically pick his jaw up off the floor at T.J.'s kindness. Noah looked at Isaac who made eyes at him. Eli did the same. Yeah, the three of them were on the same page, all right.

"I'd be happy to." Mrs. Johnson sat next to Marianne, who pretty much knew everyone in town on a first-name basis, so it was no surprise when the two of them began to chat.

T.J. picked up the lasagna and passed it over to Mrs. Johnson, who took a nice helping before moving the dish to the next person.

Mikayla leaned closer to Noah until she was shoulder-to-shoulder. She whispered, "I don't remember the last time I saw so much spark in my mother's eyes. I've been encouraging her to get out more and socialize. She spends too much time alone in the house now that I've moved out."

"I'll ask Marianne to add her to the guest list. Seems like we're always hosting some kind of shindig here at the ranch once the dust settles after stockyard sale weekend."

"Thank you. She'd like that a lot." Mikayla's smile was the only *thank you* he needed.

Gina was the first to stand when the meal was over. "I better get Everly into a bath."

"That goes for mine, too." Eli followed suit.

"Would you care for coffee on the front porch? The view here on the ranch is the best in Gunner." T.J.'s offer shocked the hell out of Noah. Based on the fact Isaac's jaw was practically on the rug, his brother was just as floored.

"Lovely of you to offer, but—" Before Mrs. Johnson could say no, Mikayla made eyes at her mother. "So, I guess that means I'd love to."

Marianne pushed up from the table. "I'll bring out a tray."

"I got this." T.J.'s voice almost sounded like he was scolding her. "I'm capable of bringing out a few mugs of coffee. How about you take Mrs. Johnson out front to the porch."

It was Noah's turn to let his jaw drop to the floor. People changed. The concept wasn't new. But their father didn't seem capable.

Isaac leaned over to Noah. "Can I speak to you out back?"

Noah checked with Mikayla and got the nod of approval he waited for. "I'll be right out."

Isaac acknowledged both of them before taking his fresh mug of coffee outside.

Mikayla walked over to the sink and poured a glass of water. "That was the nicest dinner I've had in a long time."

Noah walked up behind her and she leaned against his chest. He wrapped his arms around her. "I could get used to having you here."

"Yeah? Maybe I'll take you up on your offer to board Prissy. That way, you'd be forced to see me."

"Give it some serious thought. We could ride together." Noah kissed her at the base of her neck. Her at the ranch? No complaints from him.

"I will."

"Good. Are you okay in here while I see what Isaac wants to talk about?"

"Right as rain."

When Noah walked outside, Isaac stood looking at the expansive night sky, mug in hand.

"Think he's dying?" Noah referred to their father as he joined Isaac out back.

"Your guess is as good as mine." Isaac shrugged his shoulders. "It was my first thought, too."

"I'm not one to stick around Casa Grande, but I don't recall seeing any women around. Him settling down with a woman was my second thought."

"We're on the same page." Isaac shifted his gaze to the sky. "Guess we'll know soon enough."

"I overheard him and Marianne whispering on the porch earlier. Think she knows?"

"It's possible. I have seen the two of them together quite a bit since being back." Isaac looked east.

"Looks like you and Gina have settled into the main house. Have you decided how long you're planning to stick around the ranch?"

"I'm thinking of building. It might be time for me to join my family on the ranch." Isaac turned to face Noah. "What do you think of the idea?"

"I can't think of a better person to have at my side than my brother."

"The whole cattle ranch thing has never been my forte. You already know that. I'm not sure how to best contribute."

"You're handy. I've personally never met a man who was more resourceful. There's plenty of work for someone with skills."

Isaac's smile faded into something more serious as he looked toward the direction of the now-empty house his twin had built for his small family. "Think Liam will come back for T.J.'s big announcement?"

"He swore he'd never set foot here again."

"True. I've seen bigger miracles lately." Isaac was right.

Noah chuckled. He couldn't help himself. "The original ironman himself seems to have been made from bendable metal. It only took sixty-seven years to surface."

"He seems genuine." Isaac had changed since reuniting with Gina and becoming Everly's father. There was something more settled about him, calmer. Happier.

"Like you said. Miracles."

∼

"Mind if I join you?" T.J.'s voice startled Mikayla.

"Not at all." She turned toward the table where he motioned for the two of them to sit down.

"How are you?" The sincerity in his eyes touched her. She'd heard a few rumors about the Quinn family upbringing. T.J. Quinn was legendary in Gunner and pretty much all of Texas in cattlemen circles for his non-traditional rise to success. Based on her conversations with Noah, a different picture of the man emerged. One who'd kept a heavy hand with his children—children who needed a father after their mother had died.

"I've had a lot coming at me in the past twenty-four hours." She saw no reason to candy-coat the truth. "Having Noah by my side has meant the world to me. I don't know what I would've done if he hadn't shown up and rescued me."

The warmth radiating from T.J. caught her off guard. "I'm sorry for what you've been through. If there's anything I can help with I'd appreciate it if you'd let me know."

"Thank you." Those were the only two words she could think of but they weren't nearly enough to express her true gratitude.

"How is Noah?" He was asking her?

"He's good." From everything she could tell.

"I hope I'm not out of line in speaking my mind." He seemed to think about his next words carefully before speaking.

"Please do." She'd take a direct person over someone who smiled to her face and talked behind her back any day of the week.

"There's something different about Noah when he's with you."

Her cheeks must've flushed because he added, "I apologize if I'm embarrassing you."

"No, it's okay." She weighed how much she should share. "I'm pretty keen on him, too."

T.J. clasped his hands together and placed them on top of the wooden table. "I've spent most of my life building a legacy for family. All I could think about was building Quinnland."

"You've built one of the most successful cattle ranches in Texas, sir."

"Please. Call me T.J."

She nodded and smiled.

"Along the way, I forgot one important detail. I read a quote by Charles Kettering recently that's been keeping me awake at night. It said, 'Every father should remember one day his son will follow his example, not his advice.'"

As much as Mikayla wanted to argue or offer words of encouragement, the feeling she had from Noah about his father didn't contradict the statement.

"I read that on the back of a magazine at the doctor's office." T.J. took a sip of his coffee. "It hit home and I've been losing sleep over it ever since. I don't know what my legacy will be when I'm gone. Maybe a man or woman isn't supposed to know. You do the best you can in a lifetime and hope it's enough for those you leave behind to remember you by. I should've given my boys more good memories with me."

"I don't know much about your past with your sons, but they are good men." She could say that with conviction. "Every single one of them turned out pretty great."

"Wasn't my doing. Marianne deserves the credit. My boys don't even want to be in the same room with me."

"Seems like you're taking steps to change that."

He nodded. "I appreciate your honesty."

Noah and Isaac walked in through the back door. T.J. stood and grabbed his coffee mug off the table. "I meant what I said. If there's anything I can do to help, it would be an honor."

Noah took a couple of steps into the kitchen. His voice broke and he froze. Isaac glanced over, gave a nod toward Mikayla and kept walking.

With a wink, T.J. said, "Remember what I said."

She wasn't sure which part of the conversation he referred to but agreed.

"Ready?" Noah seemed a little shell-shocked at seeing the two of them locked in deep conversation.

"Yes." She shouldered her handbag and joined him on the other side of the room.

He motioned toward the empty chairs around the table.

"What was that all about?"

"Your father wanted to know if there was anything more he could do to help." She'd been just as surprised as Noah seemed.

"Maybe people really can change," Noah mumbled.

She hoped so. For all their sakes.

11

Mikayla bit back another yawn. That made three on the short walk to the Jeep. Exhaustion hit hard now that she had a full belly. And now she knew that her mother was safe.

"My place is half an hour drive from the main house." Noah stopped and turned around. He studied her. "You can be showered and in bed by then if we stay here."

"I didn't think you'd stay in the main house. Ever." She couldn't cover her surprise or the fact that she was touched by the gesture. Having dinner there seemed to be a huge step for him. "You shouldn't be uncomfortable on my account."

He tugged at her hand. "Come on. You need sleep. I have a bedroom here. Or, at least I did."

The sexy little smile that tugged at her heartstrings was back. She could look into his sky-blue eyes all day. "I could use a soft pillow. The bed doesn't even have to be great. I think I could fall asleep in a chair sitting up right now and be happy."

"Then, we're staying."

The house was quiet. Mikayla followed Noah up the back staircase off the kitchen hallway, upstairs, through a game room the size of the house she grew up in, and to an impressive suite.

A massive California king bed anchored the room. There was the usual furniture, night stand and lamp on either side. The headboard looked like it was made of oak logs. A dresser and closet door covered one wall and a study desk was pushed up against the window. The direction of this view would be the backyard. There was a Noah-sized chair in the corner.

"You grew up here?" She wasn't sure she'd ever be able to leave if this had been her childhood home. It was more than nice furniture, housed inside well-decorated walls. The whole place was warm and charming, and all Noah.

Granted, when T.J. walked into a room the air cooled. The effort he was making now might not be able to make up for the past. At least he seemed genuine in his vow to change.

"We have this wing to ourselves. Eli's room used to be the one next door to mine. The twins were down the hall opposite each other. The rest of my brothers were on the other side of the house. But they spent more time over here than in their own spaces."

He showed her a massive bathroom, complete with all the essentials including fresh towels.

"How about one of my old T-shirts to sleep in?" He pulled one from his dresser and handed it to her. It would fit like a dress on her but she didn't mind.

"Works for me."

"Spare toothbrushes are in the drawer next to the sink. Help yourself."

Mikayla closed the bathroom door, showered and re-emerged clean and feeling like she could drop fifteen minutes later.

"That was fast." Noah, shirt off, was relaxed in the chair.

"I'm just that tired." She forced her gaze from his muscled chest. Instead, she glanced around the room and searched for a distraction. *Any* distraction. She noticed the bed had been turned down. She was also keenly aware of the fact she wore nothing underneath the T-shirt. And, though it fell way past her thighs, she had never been more cognizant of just how naked she was.

"The bed's yours."

"Where will you sleep?" She'd brushed her teeth and then ran a hairbrush through her wet locks. It'd take more than that to tame those wild curls that normally framed her face.

"There's a bed in the adjacent room. It's good enough for me."

She shot him a look. "I'm not kicking you out of your own bed, Noah."

He hesitated on his way to the bathroom. "I don't own a pair of pajamas."

Her throat went a little dry. Okay, a lot dry. She tried to form a word but all that came out was, "Oh."

He laughed a low rumble from deep in his chest. "Told you I'd scare you."

"I'm not afraid of you." She would probably regret this later when her heart was shattered but...

"Stay in here with me."

"You sure about that?" The husky sound to his voice warmed her in places that didn't need waking up. Not tonight anyway. Not with everything that had happened to her. And especially not because her body responded a little too readily to him.

"A hundred percent."

"I can throw on a pair of boxers." The almost naked image of him threatened to make sleep difficult with him anywhere in the vicinity and especially lying next to her.

"This bed is huge. There's plenty of room. Besides, I'll probably be asleep before you're finished in the shower."

Noah nodded and disappeared into the bathroom. She heard the shower water turn on. And not much else.

∼

A QUICK, cool shower hit the mark for Noah. By the time he brushed his teeth and climbed in bed, Mikayla's steady breathing said she was asleep. He stuck to his side of the bed, giving her a wide berth. It was more for him than her. The thought of her bare skin underneath his T-shirt stirred him in places best left alone tonight.

Sleep didn't claim him immediately, so he ran over the facts of the case in his head a few more times. The notion Bode might still be in town didn't sit right. The man was up to something. Then there was Miguel Cerano from the coffee shop. Noah frequented the place and it was entirely likely he walked out without his cell phone.

The connection to Noah's cell phone and Bode wasn't as clear. Could Bode have happened on to it at the coffee shop? Noah didn't remember seeing Bode and that would be too much of a coincidence. It felt forced and Griff had always said the evidence tells the story.

As far as motive goes, Bode was a lock. No question. The coffee shop worker could have let his interest in Mikayla turn into an obsession. That was another definite possibility. The man had means, motive and access.

But it had only been twenty-four hours and living around cousins, and an uncle who worked in law enforcement had taught Noah an investigation could change course faster than a Texas tornado.

Mikayla rolled toward him until she cuddled into his side. He had no intention of taking advantage of the situation but damned if her silky skin pressed against him didn't stir a reaction.

It was shaping up to be one helluva long night.

Noah may have dozed off once or twice but real sleep wasn't in the cards. By the time the sun peaked through the windows the next morning, he was restless. Most mornings he'd have long been awake by now.

Peeling Mikayla's arm off his chest, he slipped out of bed and then fired off a few push-ups to get the blood moving. Stomach crunches were next followed by a couple of jumping jacks to get his blood pumping. He stretched out his arms and yawned.

After throwing on a pair of jeans, he checked on Mikayla. Her arms sprawled out, she covered a good chunk of the bed. Her wheat-colored hair spilled over the white pillow cover in long waves. Seeing her there in his bed put a chink in the armor he'd shown to the world for so long.

Her sleep was deep enough that he figured he had plenty of time to grab a piece of toast and a fresh brew. He picked up his cell and checked the screen. No new messages from Griff, which also meant Bode hadn't been picked up by a deputy yet.

Then again, it was early. Griff had to know Mikayla was exhausted. His cousin might've decided not to reach out unless there was a major development in her case.

Making his way downstairs, Noah called Griff. His cousin answered on the second ring.

"You sound like you haven't slept." Griff's voice always had a deeper tone when he didn't get any shut-eye.

"I'll rest when I know Gunner is safe."

"Noble sentiment but even Hercules had a weakness. You're not a machine." Noah pointed out.

Griff bit back a yawn. "I've been driving around in search of Bode."

"I'm guessing he didn't answer when you called yesterday." Noah entered the kitchen and located a loaf of bread. He popped a slice into the toaster.

"Nope. Based on how quickly the call went to voicemail, he either shut the phone off or ran out of battery."

Noah worked on the coffee machine next after rubbing his eyes. Standing at the kitchen window, he looked out onto the expansive backyard. "Any chance he could be on the property?"

"You know as well as I do how many vulnerable spots there are at Quinnland. The house area should be safe."

"What's your gut tell you on this case?" Noah wanted to know Griff's instincts and it might help for his cousin to bounce ideas off Noah.

"Bode didn't have access to your phone."

"He's acting guilty as sin."

"Which isn't helping his case. I'd get a better feel for what's going on with him if he came in to my office." Griff's instincts had been honed by years of law enforcement work under his father, Noah's Uncle Archer.

"I keep retracing my steps. There are only three places I go on a regular basis, the coffee shop, the barn, and the feed store."

"You always lock up your Jeep?"

Noah didn't have to think about the answer to that question. "No."

Point made.

"The only reason I lock my vehicles is because of my job. I'm liable to have sensitive information about a case on a notebook in my front seat. That, and the fact I have firearms."

"I suppose anyone could've taken advantage of my unlocked door. It's not unlike me to stick my cell in the console or a cup holder when I go inside a building." In fact, Noah only kept the thing around for emergencies when he went into town.

"My instincts tell me this crime is something the perp has been contemplating for a long time. An opportunity came up and he capitalized on it."

"Using me."

"And he had to act fast to make it believable."

"How did he know she would show?" Noah had been trying to figure that out on his own.

"He baited her first."

"We had a fight at the coffee shop the other day. If this was Cerano, he was there." Noah paused. "Well, not exactly a fight so much as she walked in, saw me, and huffed out before I could speak to her."

"Unless Bode was there somewhere following her, which I can't rule out."

"Has Cerano turned up?"

"His manager said he hasn't called in sick today. His shift starts in half an hour. I plan to be there waiting for him if he shows." It was too late for Noah and Mikayla to join Griff. By the time she woke and they drove to the coffee shop the interview would already be underway.

"Let me know if you find anything out." Noah wanted to keep Mikayla as far away from the investigation today as he possibly could.

"Will do. Bode hasn't shown for work today."

"Sickness seems to be going around lately."

"Sure does."

"In an unrelated note, did you hear about our fathers talking again?"

"No." T.J. was full of surprises at the moment. "When did this happen?"

"Recently. My father came down to my office and his cell rang. He looked at me like he was confused so I read the screen. Sure enough, Uncle T.J.'s name was there plain as day."

"Did you find out what he wanted?"

"My father took the call, excused himself to the break room. When he returned, he said his brother said he wanted to open the lines of communication between them."

"The two most competitive men in Gunner, who haven't spoken in the better part of twenty years, are burying the hatchet?" All kinds of thoughts raced through Noah's mind. The loudest wondered if his father had some kind of terminal illness. "And your father didn't say what mine wanted?"

"Strange timing. Your dad asked his sons to come home for a big announcement. At the same time, he seems to be trying to reconnect with local family."

"Has he called any of your brothers?" Griff had four brothers, all of whom worked in law enforcement around the state of Texas. The apples didn't fall far from the tree in that family. T.J. had only managed to get two ranchers out of his seven boys. Three now that Isaac was home and intended to work the family business.

"Not that I know of. I'm tempted to reach out, though."

"Let me know if you do." Noah ended the call, took a couple sips of coffee and made quick work of his toast. A thought struck that perhaps he was on the wrong path to figuring out who'd abducted Mikayla. It was most likely his frustration talking, trying to convince him they were on the wrong track and getting nowhere.

Griff had narrowed down the suspects to two, Bode and Cerano. Both suddenly became ill when each of their names came up in connection with the investigation.

Bode's actions yesterday were troubling. But did they signal he was involved?

He was involved in *something*.

"Hey there." Mikayla's voice pulled him out of his heavy thoughts.

He had to admit he liked the sound of her voice first thing in the morning.

Turning around, seeing her standing there in his family's kitchen in his T-shirt made another chink in his armor. He walked over to her, cupped her face in his hands and kissed her.

"Mmm. You taste like dark roast."

He smiled as she looped her arms around him and pressed her body flush with his. The thin cotton material was all that kept them from being skin-to-skin.

"You should walk around without a shirt on more often." She beamed and those thick-lashed cobalt eyes blinked up at him.

"I'll take that under consideration, but I'm pretty sure the men in the barn won't see it the same way." Her smile made his corny remark worth it.

"Can't have you working outside in the cold like this, I guess." She pressed up to her tiptoes and kissed him, deeper this time.

He dropped his hands to her waist, one splayed against the small of her back.

One word came to mind when his lips pressed to hers. *Home.*

12

Mikayla didn't want to spoil the lighter mood by asking about the investigation. The distraction of being at the ranch was a welcomed change from the stress of what had happened. She'd spent a very long twenty-four hours analyzing the event from every angle; her brain cramped last night from thinking about it so much.

The other problem was that it didn't feel like they were any closer to figuring out who'd abducted her. Of course, that wasn't entirely true and she needed to remind herself of the fact progress was being made. A couple of suspects had been ruled out. The list of possibilities had been narrowed down. And yet, she didn't feel like they were any closer to nailing the bastard.

Pushing those thoughts out of her mind, she refocused on the man in front of her. There was so much to like about him, not the least of which was how gorgeous he was. "You're a pretty man, Noah Quinn."

He chuckled and she could feel the rumble in his chest. The freefalling sensation took away her stomach. Her heart thundered in her chest and her pulse quickened.

"*You*. You're the beautiful one. Inside and out. I mean it." The sincerity in those blue eyes of his made her want to believe him. Compliments used to make her blush; not his, not now. It could be the way he spoke them or the honesty in his gaze but she believed he meant every word.

A thunderclap of need overtook her. Mikayla couldn't remember the last time she'd made love to someone or had thoroughly been made love to. Her body screamed *too long*. She couldn't be anywhere near Noah without electricity humming through her body and she knew on instinct sex with him would be a reality-altering experience.

Of course, she'd be ruined for making love to anyone else. She was certain of that. There was something about the ease she felt with Noah that made her feel like, for the first time in her life, she could really let go with someone.

Every person she'd dated in the past had mentioned how easy it had been for her to put up a wall between them when a disagreement came up in the relationship. At least one of her exes had made a remark about her leaving her running shoes at the door when she stayed over his place.

It shocked her to realize this was the first time she'd slept in someone else's bed. And she'd slept last night. Hard. It also occurred to her that Noah might not have. "Did you get any sleep?"

"Not with you curled up to my side."

"I did that?"

He nodded and that devilish grin returned that was so good at making her knees weak.

"Best sleep I've had in longer than I can remember," she teased. It was true. She'd blame it on her exhaustion or the events from the night before but being with Noah had made her feel safe.

Another kiss obliterated what was left of her self-discipline. "Take me back to bed."

Noah stood there for a long moment, looking into her eyes and his gaze was so intense she was pretty damn sure he could see right through her. "You sure that's what you need?"

"No. But it's what I want." The fact that she needed it, *needed him* scared the hell out of her.

"You should know that I don't do *casual affairs*."

She locked onto his gaze and, meaning every word of it, said, "Neither do I."

"Good." The one word was all it took. She picked up his coffee cup and took a sip before setting it down. Then, she turned around and walked toward the stairwell. "I'll be upstairs."

Noah was behind her so fast her heart almost couldn't catch up. He ushered her the rest of the way upstairs and closed the door behind them. He took her by the wrists, linked their fingers and held her hands against the back of the door.

The move thrust her breasts toward his muscled chest and obliterated any last shred of reason she had. Her body ached for more as he moved against her, the denim unable to mask his erection.

His lips crashed down on hers and his tongue moved at a dizzying pace. There was so much hunger and need in the kiss that her knees threatened to buckle. With her back pressed against the door, she wrapped her legs around his midsection.

The low growl he released fueled her even more. She liked the feeling of control she had over his tension-filled body. She liked the way he responded to her movements. And she liked how much he reacted to her lightest touch. He slid his hands down to her bottom and his fingers, rough from working the ranch, dug into her hips as she rocked her sex against him.

His body stiffened as need coiled low in her belly. Electric impulses hummed through her, leaving a fiery trail. All she could think about was how much she needed to feel him moving inside her.

His kisses tasted like peppermint toothpaste and dark roast coffee, her new favorite combination. His spicy scent drove her to distraction. Need rocketed through her, powering her movements as she brought her hands down to roam his broad shoulders. Her fingers mapped every muscle like this was the last time she'd ever touch him.

And who the hell knew what tomorrow would bring?

After facing the possibility of what might have happened if Noah hadn't shown when he did, every fiber of her being needed to seize this moment. She needed to stop being so careful with everything she did even if the feeling didn't last, and it wouldn't. She needed to let him into her heart even if he broke it tomorrow. Because she needed to feel alive again. And she wanted to feel it with Noah.

"You're so damn sexy, Mikayla. We need to slow this down or it'll be over before it really gets good." His voice came out in a rasp.

Mikayla smiled as she scraped her teeth across his bottom lip. The knowledge she was having the same effect on him that he was having on her was a powerful drug.

"What if I like doing this?" She nipped at his lip again and she could feel his muscles tense under her fingertips.

Those sky-blue eyes darkened underneath the thickest black lashes. Damned if her heart didn't take a hit when those blues landed on her.

"If you're planning to play with fire, you should be more careful." He turned and stalked toward the bed. His movements had the athletic grace of a panther as he set her down in one fluid motion. Her hands flew to the hem of his T-shirt she wore. She lifted up the cotton T and had it over her head and onto the floor in two seconds flat.

Her hands joined his on the snap of his jeans, which were off and piled on the floor a few seconds later. He stood there in front of her. Three words came to mind. Hard. Glorious. Male. She reached out to touch him. His body was pure silk over steel. The ripples of muscles on his abdomen alone were swoon-worthy. Taking in the total package all at once caused her heart to stutter.

"Noah Quinn, you have a beautiful body." It wasn't like her to be so bold but this was Noah. Being with him, naked, felt like the most natural thing.

His face broke into a wide smile. "*You* are sexy. Jesus, those curves are driving me insane."

"I want you to touch me, Noah. I want to feel you moving inside me. And I don't want to wait."

His smile turned devilish. "There's no reason to rush a good thing, sweetheart. And I have no plans for this to be over anytime soon."

Her heart wished he meant those words about more than the heat of what was happening between them in the moment. For now, she couldn't care. All she could do was focus on him and how he made her feel. Sexy. Beautiful. Wanted.

And when he kissed her, her bones melted against him.

He pulled back enough to say, "Hold that thought while I grab something from my nightstand."

"I can't get pregnant." She blurted the words before she had a chance to think.

"Neither can I." His joke made her smile despite herself.

"I'm serious. You can get a condom if you're worried about something else but there's no need to be concerned about an inconvenient pregnancy." Now her heart really battered her chest. She'd never told a soul about her diagnosis. Not even her mother. And when she really thought about it, ever since the doctor had uttered the words stage four endometriosis, she'd felt alone.

This was the absolute worst time to bring it up, but part of her also needed him to know there was no use thinking about anything more than a short-term fling with her. Noah was a family man. He deserved a family of his own someday. She would never be able to give it to him. Ever.

He took a seat next to her on the bed; his expression turned intense. "I'm starting to fall for you, Mikayla, but I don't know where this relationship is headed yet. I can tell you in good faith that I have a clean bill of health and I haven't had sex since I got the last clearance. I haven't been around a woman I like as much as I like you in longer than I can remember. It's highly possible that I haven't felt this strong of a connection with any other person. Say this thing happening between us is the real deal. Say we decide to go into it for the long haul. I can promise I would never love you any more or less for your ability or inability to have a child. There are so many ways to start a family. You getting pregnant and carrying a child is only one of them."

He brought his hands up to cup her face as she straddled him.

"All of that's the truth? It's really how you feel?"

"I'd swear on a Bible if one was handy, but I'd rather be doing something else right now." He dropped his hands to her hips and his fingers gripped her as she took his shaft in her hand and guided his tip inside her.

A few strokes was all it took for him to swing her around onto her back, while she wrapped her legs around his midsection. All she could do was give in to the sensations flooding her as he drove himself deeper toward her core.

All she could think was how well the two of them fit as he rocketed her toward the edge. The rhythm started slow as she grabbed for purchase, anchoring herself as need built inside her at a fever pitch.

"Jesus, you feel incredible." The words came out in a low growl as he quickened the pace. She matched him stride for stride as they rose to dizzying heights.

All she could think was *more*. All she wanted was *more*. All she needed was *more*.

Noah thrust his hips harder and faster until the coil inside her released and she flew over the edge. When every last spasm drained from her, he moved at a steady and mind-blowing pace. Knowing he built to his own peak, she wriggled him in deeper as he growled her name. His own climax released with a primal grunt that stirred those same butterflies in her stomach.

Mikayla was in deep trouble with this man.

NOAH DIDN'T MOVE. Couldn't move. Didn't want to move. He didn't want to break apart any faster than he had to. His heart beat staccato inside his chest, pounding his ribs. Jesus, he was done for.

Granted, he hadn't had sex in a while, not that he hadn't had plenty of offers. And he hadn't had great sex in longer than he could remember, though he was pretty sure he'd had it a time or two. But this had been mind-blowing, body consuming orgasmic bliss.

The connection between him and Mikayla was insanely strong. A definite first for him to be falling so fast and so hard. Was he ready to take a ride that could end with his heart being stomped on?

He leaned toward Mikayla as he tried to catch his breath, keeping most of his weight on his elbows and knees. Her breathing was just as uneven when he slowly pulled out and rolled onto his side.

"Everything okay?" She was quiet. Too quiet.

"Better than that."

He cracked a smile. "Amazing?"

"I could go that far."

"Best sex of your life?" Now, he really was teasing her into a compliment.

She rolled onto her side to face him and said, "You weren't bad."

"Bad and sex don't belong in the same conversation with my name." He feigned indignance.

"You were good. Probably great by most standards." If she hadn't been smiling ear-to-ear when she spoke, he might be offended.

"Are you challenging me for round two?"

"Take it to mean whatever you want, cowboy." She kissed him and that was all it took to get him hard again.

This time, he made slow love to her.

∽

The sun was bright in the sky. Noah had put off the day as long as he could, but after another round of sex in the shower, he figured Mikayla would be hungry. "I'll rustle up breakfast. Come down when you're finished showering."

"I'm starving. And coffee sounds like heaven right now." The water cut off as Noah left the room and headed downstairs.

It was late by a rancher's standards, so seeing T.J. in the kitchen standing next to the sink with a glass of water in one hand and what looked like pills in the other caught him off guard.

T.J. tossed the pills back and took a swig of water. When he set the glass on the counter he noticed Noah walking into the room. He seemed just as caught off guard as Noah.

"I thought I saw your Jeep this morning." T.J. wore pajama bottoms and a T-shirt. Noah didn't think he'd ever seen the man looking so casual.

"It was late. Mikayla was tired. I figured it was best to stay overnight in the main house. That all right?" Noah walked to the fridge, trying to act casual about the fact he was having a normal conversation with his father. There was a first time for everything.

"Sure. Stay at the main house anytime you want. You have that whole wing to yourself." T.J.'s answer came a little too quick. He sounded like a man who was trying a little too hard. Or out of his comfort zone. His hospitality toward Mikayla went a long way toward easing some of the tension Noah felt when his father was in the same room.

If T.J. could make an effort, so could Noah.

"Much appreciated, sir."

T.J. seemed to tense at the formality. Hell, it was the way Noah had been trained to address his father since childhood.

"How'd she sleep?" T.J.'s genuine-sounding concern was another shock. Noah was too late to get a look at the pills his father had swallowed but he was becoming concerned about the man's health.

"She was able to get a good night in."

T.J. nodded and started toward the opposite hallway toward his own ground floor suite. "Good. She'll need her strength."

"This is the first time I've seen you in this room at this time of day. Are you taking the day off?" Noah's father never missed the four-thirty barn meeting considering he was the one who called them in the first place.

"I have some paperwork in my office to attend to." When Noah really looked at his father, the man did seem like he'd lost a few pounds. Were those dark circles under his eyes?

T.J. never slept in. And staying inside to do paperwork sounded like his worst nightmare. So, why did he seem casual as the day is long?

"Heard you've been trying to help out the greenhorn," T.J. stopped long enough to say.

"I hope someone can break through to him. At this point, I don't care who."

"Can't save 'em all. But that doesn't mean we can't try."

"Heard he got himself into some trouble with Dakota."

T.J. nodded. It was early in the day, but he looked tired. "You heard from any of your brothers on when they might come home?"

Had he just changed the subject? "No one seems able to get a response from Liam. Phoenix will be here as soon as he can free himself up from work. He's looking for a hole in his schedule. Cayden and Aiden are doing their best. You sure about waiting for everyone to be under one roof again before telling us what's on your mind?"

"I am. There was a time when I thought it would take a miracle to get everyone here under one roof. I've never put much creed in miracles. Yet, here you and I stand in the kitchen, talking like men. I guess I'm starting to be a believer." With that, T.J. excused himself.

By the time Mikayla joined Noah, he had managed a couple of egg sandwiches. After a kiss that threatened to get him going sexually again, he handed her a fresh mug.

"Be careful, cowboy. I could get used to this." She beamed at him. His heart took another hit. Damned if he didn't feel the same way.

"Breakfast isn't much. Eggs are good protein." Noah realized he'd left his temporary phone sitting on the counter. He reminded himself to keep better track of it as he joined Mikayla at the table.

"I had no idea you were so handy in the kitchen."

"Marianne would've done everything for us if we'd let her. She still would to this day if I didn't fuss at her. I like being independent, knowing I can take care of myself."

"You're not so bad at taking care of others." She cleaned her plate and stretched her legs. "Want to get some fresh air?"

"Marianne washed your clothes early this morning." The bathrobe she'd put on was just enough to cover her curves.

"I'll have to make sure and thank her later for that and everything else." She stood and took her plate to the sink.

"Don't worry about washing that. Just set it on the counter."

"You're just spoiling me now."

He walked up behind her and wrapped his arms around her. She leaned against his chest and he nuzzled his face into her thick, curly mane. "That's the idea."

The sound of a throat being cleared behind them got their attention.

13

"Don't mind me. I'm just getting a refill." Marianne kept her gaze to the floor as she entered the room.

"Come on in." Noah chuckled. He couldn't help himself when he got a look at Marianne's flaming cheeks.

"Spring sure has put love in the air in this house." Marianne mumbled the words and Noah could barely make them out. But he laughed again as soon as he did. Between Isaac reuniting with the love of his life and now Noah with Mikayla deepening their connection, he couldn't argue her point.

"Thank you for washing these." Mikayla smiled. "I'll run up and get dressed. Be right back."

Maybe there was something to the whole spring bringing out the lovebirds bit. The minute she left the kitchen he missed her. Hadn't he gone all mush in a hot minute?

Noah also remembered Marianne's rule about no bare skin in her kitchen and he was presently without a shirt.

"Don't say it. I'm already heading upstairs." His warning was met with a flash of eyes. Marianne was amused.

"I'm glad you finally remembered."

His cell vibrated on the counter as he passed by.

"Hey, Griff. What's going on?"

"Cerano just turned himself in at my office. I'm headed there now to interview him. Thought you'd want to stop by with Mikayla."

"We're on our way." Noah ended the call and charged upstairs. Mikayla was sitting on the bed pulling on one of her socks when he blasted into the room faster than a buck with the scent of a hunter on its heels.

One look at his face caused Mikayla to shoot to her feet. "What is it? What happened?"

"Miguel Cerano just turned up at Griff's office. He's headed there now and wants us to join him."

"Did he say anything about why?"

"Not a word. We'll find out what Cerano's up to at the same time as him if we get there in time."

The Jeep was parked next to the house and Noah was in the driver's seat, with Mikayla next to him, in a matter of minutes. The twenty-minute drive to the sheriff's office was quiet. Tension filled the vehicle. Facing the man who had a fixation on Mikayla was clearly weighing heavy on her mind.

In the parking lot, Noah cut off the engine and turned toward her. He reached over and squeezed her hand in a show of support. "Ready?"

"As much as I'll ever be." She looked at him and the hint of fear in her cobalt eyes brought out all of his protective instincts.

Noah walked around the side of the Jeep and linked their fingers. He could feel a slight tremble and he could only imagine the feelings she must be going through after what she'd been through.

Sherry greeted them in the lobby.

"We know where we're going."

"Of course you do." Sherry's compassionate smile was a warm welcome. "I'll let Griff know you've made it."

Lighting in the watch room was dim. The place was barely bigger than a decent-sized walk-in closet. The two-way mirror gave them a vantage point to see and hear everything going on in the adjacent interview room.

Cerano was five-foot-nine-inches on a good day and couldn't weigh more than a hundred and forty pounds. So Noah walked in skeptical.

Mikayla stared at Cerano, who was seated across the table. His right foot tapped against the tile and he kept shifting his hands from his lap to the tabletop and back. Cerano was average in most every way. Brown hair and eyes, pale skin. The most remarkable thing about him was the goatee that he sported, which only served to turn him into another barista. There were bags under his eyes and he had a slight cough. "The bit about being sick might not have been an excuse."

"The timing seemed off to me at first but it is April. Isn't this the high season for the flu?"

"That's right."

"He could really be sick. His skin is paler than usual and he does have the cough."

"It sounds real." Noah's hopes the man responsible for the kidnapping had turned himself in were fading fast.

"Don't think I'll ever be able to go back to that coffee shop knowing he's been secretly taking pictures of me." She shivered.

"He's a creep and he clearly has a thing for you. A low-key stalker could take the next step and try an abduction. My uncle taught us a long time ago to turn in Peeping Toms. If not caught early, they almost always escalated to rape." Accidentally leaving his phone at the coffee shop would give the jerk the opportunity he'd been looking for.

Griff entered the interview room and it looked like Cerano might vomit. Nerves?

"Miguel Cerano?" Griff would know the man's name. He had to a ask a few routine-sounding questions before he could get to the real interview.

"Yes." The guy's voice shook. Something had put a scare into him. Then again, being asked to come in for questioning in a kidnapping case of a woman he had clearly been stalking would put a man on edge.

Cerano's forwardly-hunched shoulders and awkward disposition gave Noah the impression the man didn't do a lot of dating. That might also explain the secret pictures on his cell. He didn't seem to be posting them online.

"Mind if I take a look at your phone?" Griff asked. Noah knew enough about the law to realize Griff didn't have enough on Cerano for a subpoena but that didn't mean he couldn't ask for permission.

If Cerano volunteered to let Griff take a peek, whatever he found would be admissible in court.

The guy had on a hoodie and jeans. He reached into the hoodie pouch. His expression was so awkward even Noah felt embarrassed on the guy's behalf. There was no excuse for taking pictures of a woman without her knowledge and consent. Noah had no pity there.

This kid looked like he'd just been busted passing a note in class that revealed he had a crush on a classmate. He started to pull out his phone and then stopped.

"Do I have to, like, turn this over to you?"

"Why? Do you have anything to hide?" Griff took on a conspiratorial demeanor. "Look, Miguel. I want to help you. I do. But you have to be willing to cooperate. If you're hiding something, I'll find out anyway. It's best to come clean and let me see what's on your phone. But, no, you aren't bound by law to hand it over."

Cerano shifted in his seat. The heel tapped double time. If he chewed any harder on his thumbnail it might come off.

"What if I just show you my pictures?"

"It's a start. Keep in mind the more you cooperate the more I can help you later down the road."

"I heard what happened. I didn't do anything to…I would never hurt her in any way…" The anguish in Cerano's voice was pretty damn convincing.

Mikayla crossed her arms over her chest and said, "He didn't do it."

∼

"What makes you so sure?"

"His size, for one. He's smaller than the man who carried me. I'm almost certain of that. He's sweating. Which at first, I thought meant guilt. After looking at him for a minute he looks like he's about to wet his pants."

"You don't think he's afraid of getting caught?"

"He doesn't strike me as bright enough to pull off an act like what happened. I think he's genuinely scared that he's about to be blamed for something he didn't do." The more she talked it through, the more certain she became. "Look at him, Noah. Does he strike you as someone smart enough to set me up with your texts?"

"No. He doesn't. I was thinking along the same lines. He looks like a kid who got caught skipping class and is on his third strike."

"My thoughts exactly."

"Which leaves us with Bode as a suspect." Noah brought his hands up to rest on her shoulders. She loved his physical presence behind her. She loved the feeling of connection she had with him. She loved his spicy male scent.

He was masculine and virile and the complete opposite of the nervous man sitting in the interview room. The grown man who'd surprised her, knocked her out, and dragged her into a storage box could not possibly be the kid she stared at. Being here wasn't productive.

"I'm ready to go home if you are."

"Let's do it."

On the way out, Noah explained the reason for leaving to Sherry, who nodded in agreement.

On the ride home, Mikayla's thoughts bounced around. "I don't want to believe Bode is capable of doing something this awful. I know he's up to something but I just don't think in my heart of hearts he would've done this. There was no big fight between us."

"Maybe you should call him. Try to find out what's going on."

"It's a thought. I don't want to interfere with Griff's investigation." She leaned her head back and massaged her temples. "Bode swore he didn't do it."

"I'd like to be able to take him on his word. He didn't say where he was or what he was doing and we already know he has a motorcycle."

"Which he didn't try to hide from us."

"He told us exactly how he could've gotten here. And that was a bold move on his part."

"It's obvious he's hiding something. But he was with my mother and could've hurt her. He could've used her to get to me. It doesn't make sense that he would go to her house and then leave when he was asked to if he wanted to harm me."

"We knew where he was. He could've rethought his plan when he discovered I was involved. Nothing good was going to come from him hurting your mother and I have to think on some level he must've realized it." Noah smacked the steering wheel with his flat palm. "Or he was covering for someone else."

"I don't think Bode would help someone hurt me."

"That's not what I'm saying."

"Then what?"

"He was *with* someone and had to cover it up."

"Interesting point." She figured there could be some merit to that argument. "He was giving us some kind of hint before and we didn't pick up on it."

"Agreed." Noah pulled onto Quinn property and waited as security opened the gate and waved him in. He parked the Jeep at the main house.

"I need to check on Callie."

"Can I come with you?" Mikayla loved being in the barn with him yesterday. Granted, she'd been running on adrenaline and had been tired but being with Noah in his zone was exactly where she wanted to be.

Noah's answer came in the form of a smile. He came around to her side and opened the door for her before linking their fingers. She walked beside him inside the barn.

Callie immediately jumped up and darted toward Noah. He let go of Mikayla's hand long enough to bend down and scratch his dog behind the ears. Callie wedged herself in between Mikayla and Noah.

She couldn't help but laugh. "I'm not sure she's real happy to see me."

"She'll have to get used to having another female in my life. Isn't that right, girl?" Callie ran another lap around the barn.

A noise that sounded like an object being slammed down startled Mikayla. She glanced around. "What was that?"

"I don't know." Noah scanned the area as Callie returned to Cody's side in a protective stance.

Mikayla was probably just being jumpy but she had the sudden urge to go inside the house and make sure her mother was okay. The ranch property was probably the safest place she could be. Nowhere was completely safe but this was probably as close to it as she could get.

Noah listened for a long moment. When there was no other noise, he checked on Cody before asking if she was ready.

Mikayla couldn't get out of the barn fast enough. The hairs on the back of her neck pricked. She had that creepy feeling that someone was watching her as she exited the barn. "Noah."

The crack of a bullet split the air. He turned toward her in time to see the point of impact. A shot of adrenaline pumped through Mikayla as she followed his gaze. In one fluid motion, Noah covered her with his heft. A red dot flowered on her shoulder.

Everything happened fast after that.

Men seemed to run toward them from every direction. Some of them wore cowboy hats and others had on security gear. Noah ushered her against the side of the barn.

"Make yourself as small as possible."

Mikayla crouched down on her haunches. Another bullet would have to get through Noah to get to her.

14

"Take care of her."

The security team formed a circle around Noah and Mikayla. Her unfocused gaze told him shock had set in.

"You're okay." His soothing words did nothing to break through the wall.

Noah grabbed the reins on the nearest horse, a red sorrel named after his gorgeous coat. In a blink, Noah was seated in the saddle. Since Red had just come up and was already warm, he tucked his boots in the stirrups and leaned his body weight forward over the saddle horn.

Red barreled out of the back side of the barn and toward the trees, using them as cover. Noah pulled a shotgun from the saddlebag. What was normally used against hostile and dangerous animals encroaching on the livestock would come in handy against the shooter.

A shotgun wasn't ideal. Noah would have to make do.

Gunning in the direction the shot had been fired, he considered the shooter had used a rifle. Probably something high powered. From that distance, he would've needed a scope.

The only positive was that Griff might be able to trace the weapon using a ballistic report. Noah brought the gelding so close to the tree line branches slapped him in the face.

He worried too much time had passed between the initial shot and him getting to the spot where the shooter had likely fired the weapon.

"Whoa."

Red slowed. From this vantage point, Noah scanned the area for any signs someone had just been there. The trees were too thick to walk Red through this part of the property. Security had brought up removing them for safety's sake.

This area had been staked out a long time ago and set aside for Phoenix to build his home. T.J. had figured the area would be flattened when Phoenix decided to build there. He'd nixed the idea of clearing it sooner, wanting to save as many trees as possible.

The logic had been reasonable when there was no security risk.

Noah hopped off Red and tied him off to a tree. With shotgun at the ready, he made his way through the trees with the stealth of a special operations team. There were no signs to track.

"Dammit."

Ten minutes later and no closer to finding the trespasser, Noah wound his way back to Red. In less than that, Noah handed Red off to Dakota.

"Mikayla's in the main house being looked after by Doc Graham. The bullet grazed her shoulder, so a lot of blood but it could've been a whole lot worse. All the men are out looking for the bastard who did this. T.J. is in the house about to blow a gasket."

Noah thanked Dakota for the update and took off in the direction of the main house. He saw Jess running toward him out of the corner of his eye.

"You can run with me, but I don't have time to stop and talk."

Jess's gaze was wild.

"You're okay? You didn't get hit?"

"No. I'm fine. Pissed off and ready to snap someone's neck in two maybe. But I didn't get hit."

Jess's relief was visible in his exhale. Granted, Noah was Jess's employer and according to Dakota and T.J. had reached God-like status with Jess, but his lack of concern for Mikayla rubbed Noah the wrong way. He didn't have time to educate the guy on why her taking a bullet was far worse to Noah than if he'd been the one.

Noah stopped at the back door. "Do me a favor."

"Anything, sir." Sweat poured down Jess's face. He looked frantic and that touched Noah.

"Get out there and help nail the bastard responsible. Mikayla means a lot to me and whoever hurts her might as well have put a bullet in me."

Those words seemed to hit Jess like a physical blow. All Noah had time to think about was getting to Mikayla and seeing for himself that she was okay. The thought of anything happening to her, and on his watch, made a shitty day feel it had taken another nose dive. Much more of this and the plane would explode to the ground.

Jess whispered something that sounded like *sorry* before he turned heel and took off in the opposite direction. The guy might be taking this harder than he needed to. Noah would straighten him out once the excitement settled down. For the time being he needed all hands on deck, searching for the bastard who'd shot Mikayla.

A thought struck the shooter might've been aiming for him and his mind snapped to Bode. Noah opened the back door and heard the familiar voices of his family.

T.J.'s boomed, "This is my family we're talking about, Griff. Someone trespassed on my property and hurt one of ours."

The fact his father considered Mikayla like family already struck a warm chord for Noah. The scene inside the kitchen was one of organized chaos. Mikayla was seated at the table with Doc Graham attending to her shoulder.

Marianne hovered beside Isaac, who turned when Noah entered the room.

"She's doing great." His brother's reassurance let Noah exhale a decent breath for the first time since the whole ordeal started.

Noah nodded to his brother as he passed by and moved to Mikayla's side. The color had returned to her face and her breathing resembled something normal.

"Everything happened so fast out there." Mikayla might not know it but she was a bad-ass as far as he was concerned.

What was it about the thought of losing someone, that made everything in a relationship suddenly become crystal clear?

"There wasn't much time to react." Noah took a knee beside her, opposite from the shoulder Doc Graham worked on. He glanced at the doc. "What's the damage?"

"No bullet fragments, so that's a good sign. Shrapnel nicked her shoulder. I've cleaned it up, sterilized the area and am finishing up with a couple of sutures. She's strong. She'll heal up in no time."

Another exhale came as Noah clasped their fingers. He brought her right hand up to his lips and kissed the back. And then he looked at her. "We'll nail the bastard. He won't get to you again."

T.J. stood in the center of the room, phone to his ear. "Do whatever you need to. I'll have security run the tapes over to you."

They'd be grainy as hell. They were meant to find out what kind of predator could be encroaching on the herd. A man would have to put his face directly to the camera to capture any of his features. He'd have to be standing within two feet of the lens and at the perfect angle.

The words *lost cause* didn't begin to describe going down that rabbit hole.

It was pretty obvious he could've hurt her right then and there. The notion he'd been rushed and had taken advantage of an opportunity was gaining legs. The evidence never lied.

Isaac disappeared. He returned with a laptop in hand as Doc Graham was putting a gauze pad over the wound.

"Security footage will be easy to pull up here. We can send the digital file to Griff. Max is working on getting that over right now." Isaac placed the laptop on the table, positioning it so Noah could see.

T.J. moved behind them, quietly explaining to Griff the scene as it unfolded.

Sure enough, at around two-thirty p.m. a male figure came into view on camera number three. And, sure enough, he had on a ski mask and a hoodie, making it next to impossible to make out any of his features.

The male moved through the trees, keeping his head down. The rifle in his hand looked generic enough to make it impossible to trace based on its model. The perp's baggy dark clothes made it difficult to make out his true size. He wasn't too short or too thin, and that ruled out Cerano. Those clothes would hang off the barista.

But with a description of roughly six-foot-tall with broad shoulders and better than average build the rest of the male population of Gunner between the ages of eighteen and forty-five couldn't be ruled out.

The figure looked to be wearing work gloves, too. So, there'd be no fingerprints left behind to dust.

"There isn't much here," T.J. said into the phone. "We'll send over what we have. Maybe you can do something with it."

A fresh set of eyes, especially those trained to notice little things, couldn't hurt to have on the footage.

Eli came through the back door. "Dakota thinks he caught a trail leading away from near the site of the shooter. He's been tracking him. Cell coverage is spotty on that part of the land and I lost contact with him, but he seemed pretty sure he was onto something. One of the greenhorns volunteered to back him up."

Seeing Eli was nice, but Noah knew that the information could've been relayed via a phone call or text message. The hair on the back of his neck pricked and he pushed up from the table and stood because something else was most definitely happening. "What is it? What else is going on?"

"It's Callie. Something's wrong. She's not acting right." Eli's apologetic gaze was a physical punch.

Noah glanced at Mikayla, who nodded. "I'm in good hands. Go take care of her."

Eli put his hands up to stop his brother. "This could be a trap to get you outside and exposed. We have no idea where the shooter is."

"I'll take that risk." Shooter or not, Callie needed him. Noah pushed past his brother. Eli turned on his heel and followed. T.J. joined Eli, flanking Noah on both sides.

The trio covered the distance to the barn in less than a minute. Noah ran to Callie, who was lying on her side. Her whimpers nearly gutted him as he dropped down next to her.

"You're okay, girl."

One of the ranch hands, Dale, backed up a couple of steps. "It's like she got into some poison. Except we all know we don't keep any around this part of the barn."

This area held the offices on one side and stalls on the other. There was a tack room and an equipment room that was always under lock and key. The main area was the most trafficked with ranch hands moving in and out and the location where morning meetings took place. Which also meant everyone had access.

"Get Michael on the phone." The family vet had worked with animals on the Quinn ranch for years, as did his father before him.

"Immediately, sir. He's on his way." Dale brought a fresh bowl of water to Callie.

Cody lifted his head. He seemed to realize something was wrong as he strained to get to his feet. Dale moved beside Cody, who seemed determined to get to the border collie. The black lab walked on shaky legs toward his newfound friend. He stopped next to her and dropped down like it had taken all his energy to get there.

With his back next to hers, she repositioned her head so their ears touched. It was clear she drew comfort from Cody. The scene unfolding before Noah caused his throat to dry and his eyes to gather moisture.

He cleared his throat and snapped into action.

"What the hell could he have used?" Noah immediately jumped to his feet and started looking around the open area. Half a dozen stalls were on one side of the barn and offices lined the opposite wall. "Look for anything, empty bottles. Rat poisoning."

Eli was on his feet, searching. There were plenty of poisons on a ranch. At Quinnland, there was a strict policy about storing those chemicals in a safe place and harsh chemicals were never allowed anywhere near horses or livestock. Those were supposed to be kept under lock and key. Dakota was the only non-Quinn who had access to the poison room but the person who'd stolen Noah's cell phone would be capable of taking a set of keys and returning them before Dakota noticed.

Hell, a decent thief would have the skills necessary to take something right under someone's nose and no one would be the wiser.

Noah picked through the trash can outside the stalls, looking for an empty bottle or any type of container. He thought about a book he'd read in high school, The Art of War. In war, the way is to avoid what is strong and strike at what is weak. "It has to be here somewhere."

While Dale collected samples to be given to the lab for evaluation, Eli and Noah made quick work of checking behind hay bales for empty cartons or hastily tossed plastic jugs.

"I got something here." Eli held up a pesticide bottle with a sprayer attached as the vet arrived.

"Looks like she was given pesticide." Noah ushered Michael to Callie's side.

Michael checked her over. "Has she had any seizures? Loss of consciousness? Or difficulty breathing?"

"None that I'm aware of."

"That's a good sign." He pulled a wipe from his bag and used it to clean Callie's skin and coat. "I'm going to orally administer activated charcoal to absorb any of the poison in her mouth."

Michael made quick work of it, and Callie complied. The normally on-the-go girl kept her head down like she knew Michael was there to help.

"I need to get her to my office. I want to put her on an IV to flush out her system. I'll need blood work to assess the level of toxins in her blood and see if any kidney damage has occurred."

"What's the worst case here, Michael?"

"She could need extensive therapies like dialysis, but we'll cross that bridge when we come to it. Right now, I'm hopeful all she was given was enough pesticide to make her sick. I need to run panels to see if we're dealing with any other substances."

"I'll help you get her in your truck." Noah scooped her up. She was dead weight in his arms.

"What time did this happen?"

Noah looked to Dale. "She was fine one minute. Someone had to have gotten to her in the last fifteen minutes or so."

Noah fisted his hands. "Who's been in the barn?"

"Hard to say, sir. Everyone's out on property trying to find the shooter. I came back to get my gloves and found her like this."

"What about your gloves? Did you find them?" Noah remembered the person on camera had been wearing gloves. They looked generic enough.

"No. Thought I left them right here when I checked on Cody."

First Noah's cell phone and now a pair of gloves. But what had Callie ever done to make someone poison her?

The answer struck Noah like a physical blow. "This could all be one big distraction."

Something was niggling in the back of Noah's mind and he couldn't for the life of him figure out what it was. This day had gone to hell in a handbasket pretty damn fast. All he could think was if Bode was responsible for any of this...Noah would wring the man's neck with his bare hands if he got hold of him.

"I'll head back to the main house. You stay here with Callie." T.J. was on his way out before Noah had a chance to put up an argument.

"Let him go. He wants to help." Eli stood watch over the door, giving Noah the freedom to focus on the dog who'd been his best friend for the better part of a decade.

Noah leaned down to Callie's ear as he gently placed her in the passenger seat of the truck's cab. "Keep breathing for me, girl. I'm not ready to let you go."

If it was her time or she was in pain and had no hope of getting better, that was one thing. For someone to cut her life short when she still had so much vitality was a different story. She was so much more than a cattle dog to Noah. The fact someone would hurt her to distract him set his blood to boiling.

Someone had breached the ranch. Someone had shot Mikayla. Someone had poisoned his dog.

That same someone had found, or stolen, Noah's cell phone. There weren't many people who could've had that kind of access.

Noah looked up at Eli because one word haunted him. *Sorry.*

"When was the last time someone saw Jess?"

"Right before I came to get you. Why?"

"Is he the greenhorn you sent after Dakota?"

"Yes."

15

"We need to get to Dakota before Jess does."

A shot of adrenaline had Noah up and on his feet because the puzzle pieces just clicked together in his mind. Dakota was in danger.

"You think it's him?" Eli's shock was written all over his face.

"Think about it. He has access to the barn. He's young and strong. He fits the general height and weight. More importantly, he could've taken my cell phone. I've worked around him plenty and he has to know how little I keep track of it."

"Why would he do that? For what reason?"

"I'll ask the bastard myself when I hunt him down." The amount of anger ripping through Noah was the equivalent of a volcano exploding. There'd been so many warnings that Noah had glazed right over, instead of taking serious, because he never would've expected Jess to turn on the very family who was trying to help him. But then Jess's mind wasn't right. It had been obvious from day one. He'd messed up and they'd been willing to give him second and third chances.

"Let's assemble and figure out a plan before we go running off into the woods where someone might get hurt." Eli made sense because right now Noah was running off pure emotions.

"Someone needs to stay back to protect Mikayla. It's clear Jess has targeted her and I'm guessing it's because of her association with me. There are babies here along with Gina and Marianne, all of whom need to be safeguarded. We can have them lock themselves indoors and set the alarm, but the reality is he could bust through a door and get to them." Reality set in and Noah was torn between taking off to hunt for Jess, staying with Mikayla to ensure her safety, and going to Michael's office to stay by Callie's side in case she didn't make it. He wanted to be there for her if she crossed over because, dammit, she'd been his faithful companion.

Noah couldn't pinpoint the exact moment he'd lost faith in people. It very well could've happened all those years ago when his mother had died and his father had become so angry. T.J. had loved his wife. Losing her had caused the man to cave. Noah had faint memories of a time before she'd died. It was evident to anyone in the room that T.J.'s world revolved around her. In losing her, he'd lost himself.

Or maybe losing faith in others had happened in the years that had followed when Noah had struggled with his own anger and had almost been swallowed up by that same darkness.

Mikayla was the light and all he wanted to do was move toward it, toward her.

"Horses are still saddled. I'll have Dale bring them around." Eli looked to Noah. "Kiss my kids for me. Tell them I'll be home as soon as I can."

"Will do, Eli. I'm bringing Cody to the main house for protection."

"You know T.J.'s rule about animals in the main house."

"He'll have to get over himself." Noah had already scooped Cody up in his arms. "I'll kiss your kids but wait for me, dammit. Once we get out there, cell coverage will be spotty and I don't want to lose contact. We have strength in numbers and communication; if he isolates us, we'll be fighting on his terms." Make no mistake about it, Jess had waged war on the Quinns by targeting the person Noah cared about and then his best friend. "If he divides us, he has a better chance of an advantage."

But what the hell did he hope to prove? What was he after? What was his end game?

Those and other questions hung heavy on Noah's shoulders as he carried Cody to the main house. T.J. was in the kitchen along with Mikayla, Gina, Marianne, and the kids. Mikayla's mother looked almost frantic.

"What happened?" Gina pushed up from the table and bolted toward Cody.

"Someone poisoned Callie while she was in the barn. I'm not taking any chances with him. He's too weak." Noah shot a look at T.J. practically daring him to complain about bringing the dog inside. T.J. immediately nodded his approval. It wouldn't have mattered to Noah, and yet it felt good all the same.

"I'll get blankets." T.J. started toward the hall.

"I'll go with him." Marianne jumped into action.

"Have you heard anything else about Callie? Is she going to be okay?" Mikayla was by Noah's side in a heartbeat, the expression on her face said she cared for Callie a great deal.

"God, I hope so."

T.J. and Marianne brought blankets and pillows for the dog and placed them in the middle of the room. Noah gently set the dog on top of the blanket in middle of the kitchen floor.

"Michael's working on her. He took her back to his clinic. He's hopeful we got to her in time. He won't know the extent of how much she ingested until he runs labs, which he's expediting."

"I'm so sorry, Noah. Can I go stay with her?"

He locked gazes to show her just how serious he was. "It's best if you don't leave this house at the moment."

Chin out and brave face on, Mikayla didn't respond and he could see her turmoil about whether she should stay at the ranch or be with Callie. It was easy to see in her the same emotions he was running through internally.

She took one of Noah's hands in hers and linked their fingers. "She'll be okay. She has to be."

He appreciated the warmth, the concern and the sentiment.

"I better go. Eli's waiting." He shot her a look of apology. More of the mix of emotions played across her features. Hell, he was just as torn. Torn between needing to stay put and protect Mikayla. Torn between needing to be at Callie's side. Torn between intercepting Jess and protecting Dakota.

If Jess found Dakota first, the greenhorn could end up with the upper hand. Not that Dakota couldn't fend for himself, but anyone could be ambushed or caught off guard if they didn't know what they were looking for or weren't expecting it.

And then there was Isaac, who was already out on the property out of cell range. He could walk into a trap. In a perfect world, Isaac and Dakota would be together. Both would see through Jess.

"Why can't you stay here?" Mikayla asked.

"It's Jess. He's responsible. And now he's out there looking for Dakota. Eli is bridling the horses with Dale's help; the three of us are going out together to find Dakota before Jess does."

Gina gasped. "I haven't been able to reach Isaac. He's out there."

"I know. We'll find him." He hadn't mentioned Isaac yet because he didn't want Gina to worry. A couple men from security and a handful of ranch hands were scouring the land, looking for a shooter. Word would spread about Jess.

"I'm coming with you." T.J. was stopped by Marianne's hand on his arm.

"No. You're not."

Noah had never seen Marianne react this way to his father. Surprisingly, T.J. backed down. No argument. Noah was really worried about his father now. T.J. had never been put in his place by an employee. But then, Marianne was more like family. She and Dakota had been at Quinnland over the long haul. And T.J. would do to listen to Marianne. The only reason Noah and his brothers had turned out to be good men was because of her.

"You'll be more help here." Noah threw the lifeline. "Between the three of us and the security team, we need people here at the house. I have no idea where Jess is or why he's doing this but I intend to find out."

T.J. paced around the kitchen. "I should've known. All he ever talks about is you. He's always asking where you are and what you're doing."

The notion Mikayla was in danger because of Noah sat like nails in his gut.

"Set the alarm. Call Griff. Fill him in. I need to go find Dakota."

"Be careful, son." The warmth in T.J.'s tone was a shocker.

Noah nodded before starting toward the back door with Mikayla. She tugged at his arm, so he turned to face her.

Staring into those cobalt eyes, he would never be able to refuse her, so he prayed she wouldn't ask him to stay. "Come back to me in one piece."

"I will." It was a promise both knew he might not be able to keep. He'd die trying. "There's something I need to tell you. But it'll have to wait until I get back and I *will* be back." One more kiss and Noah was out the door and headed toward the barn. He was met halfway by his brother and Dale, both of whom were already on horseback.

Eli handed over the reins to Red. Noah made quick work of hopping into the saddle. Once seated, the trio turned the horses around and started toward the woods. They used the barn as cover, giving a wide berth. Being out in the open exposed them for a long-distance shooter but shielded them from an ambush.

The only hope Noah had was that Jess hadn't tried to kill him. In fact, the greenhorn had seemed very concerned that Noah was okay when the two had spoken earlier.

Noah led the pack, charging toward the woods in hopes a shooter wouldn't get a steady shot. If Jess had become fixated on Noah, then Eli and Dale were at the greatest risk of being shot. Noah seemed to get a free pass and he had no doubt now that he thought about it that the earlier bullet had been meant for Mikayla.

"We have a basic idea of Dakota's whereabouts, but nothing is certain." Noah and his brother knew best the blind spots for cell service on the ranch from when they were younger. Even though Noah had never gotten into the technology craze, he still had an idea of where all the dead spots were based on overhearing his brothers complaining.

Plus, there were all the times he listened to them complain because they couldn't talk to one of their high school girlfriends while out riding fences before school, when everyone else gathered early in the parking lot and caught up with each other before class. He'd watched each of his brothers trying to find those elusive bars and they'd put themselves in some random places and sometimes damn funny positions.

The trio had to slow their pace considerably when they entered the woods. Being on horseback gave them a better vantage point but Jess could literally be anywhere. All the other horses were accounted for, which meant Jess was on foot. Being a war buff, Noah remembered how America's war for independence was won, the settlers hid in trees and ambushed British soldiers.

Noah was prepared for anything.

Except the sight they came upon.

16

The screech of sirens split the air. Law enforcement was on its way. Mikayla sat on the kitchen floor, her left arm basically useless. With her right hand, she patted Cody's midnight-colored coat and offered soothing words to the sweet lab.

Gina sat on the floor while the babies were playing in the guest room set up for them. T.J. and Marianne had volunteered to stay in the room with the kids. So, it was Gina and Mikayla on the floor with Cody.

A picture had emerged in the past few hours of a young ranch hand who'd become obsessed with Noah. Why the man wanted to hurt her was beyond her reasoning ability. She posed no threat. Her thoughts bounced around. There was some relief that Bode wasn't involved. He'd gotten himself into something that was causing him to hide his whereabouts but that could mean many different things.

Noah was out there, somewhere, trying to stop a maniac from striking an innocent human and she felt completely useless inside the main house while she did nothing to help him.

Isaac was only God knew where at this point.

"This family has been through a lot recently." Gina's sincerity and warmth was a flood to dry plains. Gina had been two years ahead of

Mikayla in school. She didn't know her except to know of her. It seemed everyone in Gunner knew a few details of each other's lives.

And Mikayla didn't realize until recently how alone she'd become in Gunner once all her friends left. The diagnosis had only made her feel worse. Her eyes were also opening to the fact that her life had shrank to a very few people she stayed in contact with after they'd moved.

Leaving Gunner had never been a real consideration for her. And yet, it did feel like everyone in Gunner had left her.

Since she had no plans to leave, it was high time she made an effort to make new friends and she hoped like hell Gina would be one of them. "I heard about what happened to you. I'm just glad you and Everly are safe now."

Giving their present conditions, they both laughed and it broke some of the heavy tension filling the air.

Technically, no one was or would be safe until the jerk was behind bars. But if Jess went after anyone, it would be Mikayla. Anyone near her could be caught in the crossfire, though.

"Damn," she muttered when it dawned on her that her presence was putting the entire house in danger. She'd never be able to live with herself if a child ended up hurt or worse because of her. Don't even think about one of the parents being hurt.

"Don't think about leaving. It'll only make everything worse." Gina's promise rang true in Mikayla's ears, and yet she couldn't reconcile putting so many lives in danger when all Jess really wanted was her.

"Wouldn't everyone be better off if I was somewhere else?"

"Not even close."

"How did you know what I was thinking, by the way?" Mikayla didn't bother to mask her surprise.

"I've been in your shoes, remember. Isaac was jumping into the line of fire for me. He could've had a free pass. But that's not the way Quinn men are built." Gina didn't seem to be judging, just commenting on truths she'd learned the hard way. Warning Mikayla in the way a big sister might.

If anyone knew what Mikayla was going through, it was Gina. She'd unwittingly come upon a murder scene, was abducted and then targeted for murder by one of their childhood classmate's new stepfather, Bo Stanley. He had a criminal history for ripping off women, which he'd managed to hide from the murder victim's mother when he'd conned her into marrying him. The man was a class-A jerk. He was locked behind bars, awaiting a trial which most in the state believed would be a slam dunk. Justice would be served.

"You, Isaac, and Everly make a sweet family."

Gina thanked Mikayla. "If we have anything to say about it, we'll be a family of four soon. We want Everly to have a sibling close in age."

Mikayla dropped her gaze.

"What's wrong? Did I say something?"

There was no reason to confide in Gina, other than she seemed like a good person. Since most of Mikayla's friends had moved away from Gunner, she figured she could use an ally. And her heart told her she had to make a decision soon.

"It's not you or anything you said. I can't..." Mikayla couldn't even say the words.

Gina searched Mikayla's face. She seemed to catch on. "And you think Noah deserves to have a family of his own."

Her newfound friend had nailed it on the head. Wise woman. Mikayla definitely needed more strong, intelligent and intuitive women in her life.

"He doesn't think so, but I'm worried he'll wake up and regret being in a relationship with someone who can't have kids. One of these days, he's going to want a son or daughter of his own and I'll end up hurt and alone. Except that the Quinns are honorable men and he won't want to tell me why he's become so distant. He won't leave me, either. He'll live an unhappy, unsatisfied life with me."

Damn, those words had been forming in her head so long. Hearing them changed her opinion about them, took away the fear and worry. What was it about saying something out loud that seemed to take the mystique away from it? She heard how illogical the words sounded. They came from a place of pure emotion and doubt. Doubt in herself. Doubt in her ability to have a normal, honest relationship. Doubt that she'd ever be good enough for a man like Noah.

Gina leaned back on her heels. She seemed to really consider what Mikayla had to say before she decided to speak.

"The thing I've noticed about Quinn men is that they know their own minds. Every last one of them." Gina paused a couple of beats as though to let the thought really sink in. "If something bothers them, they'll come out with it. They won't leave you guessing. So, what did Noah say when you told him?"

"That he didn't care. It didn't matter to him because if we decided to have a family there were so many other ways to go about it."

"Do you think he has a point?"

"If we're going to stay together, I want to be able to give him those things. Children. A family. A home."

"What you're saying makes sense. It does. So, I won't try to sell you on another idea. He's right. There are so many other options, not the least of which is exploring you being able to carry a child. There are so many advances in medicine now."

Logically, she knew what Gina was saying was the truth. In her heart, down deep, the minute the doctor told her it was unlikely she'd ever get pregnant, she'd been letting fear rule over reason.

"You're making good points. Researchers make progress every day." It wasn't unreasonable to think by the time she and Noah decided to have a family that she would be able to conceive and carry a child full-term. The other sigh of relief came in having a true friend to be able to confide in. Mikayla liked Gina. She'd already witnessed her as a mother, and Mikayla couldn't imagine a mother who loved her child more. Gina and Isaac seemed to be head over heels in love with each other. Isaac seemed all-in as a father to Everly and it came across as the most natural thing to him. The fact Everly wasn't his biological child didn't seem to bother him one bit. If he and Gina had a biological child together, Isaac didn't seem like he'd love one more than the other.

She was pretty certain she'd overheard him saying he'd like a boy since he already had a daughter during lunch.

"Granted, I'm new to the inner workings of this family but I've never seen Noah look so happy or so at peace than when he's with you. It's easy to put up arguments in your head about why something will or won't work. Do yourself a favor. Let your heart decide."

Mikayla couldn't argue the advice. She could only hope that Noah would come back to her unharmed.

Because now that she'd found him, she couldn't imagine losing him. And if Jess had anything to say about it, she'd be out of the picture for good.

A noise sounded down the hallway. Glass breaking?

The alarm beeped a warning. It was about to blare.

Someone was in the house.

∽

THE SCENE NOAH, Eli, and Dale came upon brought all three to their knees. Dakota's still body splayed out at the base of Diamond Rock, his face covered in blood. This part of the ranch had hills, at least by Texas standards.

His horse, Ginger, was nowhere around. His tracks lead east, the direction of the main house.

In one motion, Noah dismounted Red. Dale was there in the next second taking reins so Noah and Eli could attend to a motionless Dakota.

"Try to get cell coverage, Dale." Eli barked the order. "The top of the rock. Go to the top of the rock. Call T.J. and tell him what we found."

Seeing him there, his body so still, was a gut punch. They'd all ignored the warning signs with Jess, and Dakota was paying the price. Maybe they'd gotten too cocky. Thought they could save everyone, even the direst cases. How Noah wished that was true, and not because a man who'd been like an uncle to him for Noah's entire life lie before him but because everyone deserved a decent chance at this life.

Noah dropped beside Dakota, taking the opposite side as Eli. Noah searched for a pulse. "I got one."

"We need to find the source of the blood." Eli was right. There was too much fresh blood and if Dakota lost too much his chances of survival dropped to zero. Noah felt around Dakota's head, searching for the source.

He spied a spot above Dakota's ear. Blood pulsed. "I got something. Come look."

Eli scooted around to get a better look. He pulled a bandana from his back pocket and applied pressure to the wound. "That should help. I have more in my saddlebag."

Noah jumped to his feet. "How are you coming with that signal, Dale?"

"Nothing yet."

"Keep trying." Noah retrieved a couple of bandanas from the bag and returned to his brother's side a few seconds later. He handed them to Eli who fashioned a make-shift bandage.

"That should help hold until we can get him to the main house." Eli lifted his face toward the top of the hill. "No signal yet?"

"Nothing, sir."

"Come help us get him on my horse."

Moving Dakota was taking a risk. Leaving him there was certain death. There was no choice but to give him a chance.

Eli and Noah went to either side of his torso, one arm under his back and the other under his leg. Dale took Dakota's head.

The trio managed to get him to Eli's horse and Eli mounted. "I'll have to take it easy."

Dakota shook his head, his eyes blinked open. "Mikayla. He's going after Mikayla."

Eli and Noah locked gazes.

"Go. I have this covered." It was quickly agreed that Dale would stay back with Dakota for cover.

Noah had to get to Mikayla in time. He mounted Red and they took off toward Casa Grande.

Red liked to run and it was a damn good thing under the circumstances. He barreled toward home and Noah let Red set the pace.

The minute Noah hit the clearing he heard the house alarm echo across the lawn. *Dammit.*

"Come on, Red. Get me there." Red was better than a bullet train. But Noah had no idea what kind of scene he was going to come up on when he made it to Casa Grande. He slowed Red, dismounted, and then quickly removed his bridle. He released Red in the exercise pen nearest the barn.

Noah bolted toward the house, running so fast and hard his thighs burned. His Colt revolver drawn, leading the way. Seconds might mean the difference between life and death if he came in contact with Jess.

The kid was a few cards short of a full deck and Mikayla seemed to have triggered him. Now, he was going after her. He had the advantage because he'd gotten there first. Noah slowed his pace as he neared the house. He moved to the kitchen window and peeked inside.

Cody was gone and the room was empty.

Noah moved to the bedrooms. The screech of the alarm in his ears caused a ringing noise. There was no way to listen for sounds inside the house. He had to rely on what he could see.

Another siren he recognized sounded from behind him. He turned to see Griff's SUV roaring up to the side of the house gravel spewing underneath his tires. Help was a welcomed sight.

And the distraction was even better. Noah rounded the back side of the house and slipped inside. He crouched low enough to keep his body hidden from view behind the kitchen island.

Keeping himself as small a target as possible, he moved around the side of the granite island. The sound of a door being burst open on the second level echoed. He listened for the sound of screams over the ear-piercing sirens. None came, so he held his position.

And then he heard the footsteps coming down the back stairwell.

Noah strained to listen over the annoying alarm. If he didn't have a headache from everything else that had happened so far that day, there was no doubt he would before this was over. He prayed like hell a headache was the worst of what would happen to him and those he loved.

One set of footsteps came barreling down the steps.

17

The footsteps were heavy enough to belong to a male. This had to be Jess.

Noah reminded himself to wait. Bide his time. Strike when he was certain he could take Jess down without risking injury to anyone else in the house.

His thoughts, sympathy ran deep for Dakota. The man had been nothing but nice to Jess.

Knowing Dakota, he'd shrug and say he couldn't win them all. Life at the ranch wouldn't be the same without him if he didn't make it. Noah pushed those heavy thoughts aside. Based on the noise level outside, backup had just arrived for Griff and he'd be coming through that front door in a minute.

The clomp of boots on tile flooring drew Noah's attention toward the sound.

He waited. Patience was the virtue he needed to succeed. Lucky for him, patience was his strong suit.

Hunkered as low as he could get, Noah sprang toward Jess the second he came into view. The greenhorn twisted around enough for Noah to roll a little too far, causing him to lose his balance and the advantage.

There was a small amount of blood and Noah couldn't be sure if it belonged to him or Jess.

The greenhorn aimed his gun at Noah. "Don't make me do this. I don't want to hurt you. I never wanted to hurt you. I just wanted to be your friend but she won't let me."

Noah had to think fast because this had to be coming from somewhere in Jess's past. Clearly, Mikayla would never do anything to hurt Jess.

"You *are* my friend."

"No. You chose her over me. You go spend time with her instead of me. I'm here waiting but you never show."

Noah didn't have the first idea what Jess was talking about. He couldn't remember standing the young man up...hold on. He'd stood Jess up the other morning. He'd promised to come back and talk to Jess. Granted, the greenhorn had already abducted Mikayla but that wasn't the point. Jess was already off the rails.

"She'll hurt you in the end. I had to stop her. It's happened before. You just don't know what she's capable of." Jess's adult expression morphed into that of a wounded child.

The words *I had to stop her* rang in Noah's ears.

"Jess, what have you done?"

The front door swung open. Jess hesitated and Noah saw his opportunity to subdue the guy. Noah bounded to his feet and tackled Jess. The pair landed hard on the tile floor. Noah took a damn hard blow to the head. Enough that he saw stars.

"I'm not trying to hurt you. But you can't go around hurting others, either." Noah's grip weakened after the blow. That headache would hit the minute adrenaline wore off.

"You're taking her side." Jess grunted and threw himself into a spin like an alligator disorienting its prey.

Noah held on as tight as he could. It wasn't going to be enough. He could feel Jess slipping from his grip. His thoughts went to Mikayla. She had to be upstairs and the blood on Jess might just belong to her. The staggering thought she could be somewhere in the house bleeding out shot another round of anger in Noah. Enough that he was able to hold on a little longer.

It was then Isaac blew through the back door. "Noah."

God, his brother was a welcomed sight as he literally dove on top of Jess, giving Noah enough space to roll away from the young buck. A couple of deep breaths later and Noah pushed to his feet. His head felt like it had cracked in two but he managed to stand in time to see Griff and Deputy Sayer come running from the front room.

"I have to find her," was all Noah said as he bolted toward the stairwell Jess had come from.

"Go with him. I've got this." Griff's voice floated up the stairs as he Mirandized Jess.

Damned if life hadn't been black and white to Noah before this whole ordeal. He was learning the gray area. Jess needed mental health support and Noah would make sure the kid got it. Without a doubt, Jess needed to pay for his crimes. Justice had to be served.

Noah crested the stairs in time to see Mikayla crawling toward him. She had blood on her face, her shirt.

"I need an ambulance. *Now*." He shouted downstairs.

∽

MIKAYLA ROLLED ONTO HER BACK. The sweet sight of Noah running toward her felt like a dream. She'd made it. Jess was gone. She'd saved the others, the kids.

There was banging on a door coming from down the hall.

"I did it, Noah. It's okay." She felt cold and her body started shaking.

Noah didn't smile. Instead, wrinkles creased his forehead. His beautiful face was coming in and out of focus. "Stay awake, Mikayla. Don't close your eyes."

She tried to open her mouth enough to form words but it felt like her brain had somehow disconnected from her body.

"I love you, Mikayla." Noah's hands cupped her face now. "I want to spend my life with you. When you're with me, I'm home."

I love you, Noah.

~

Noah practically had to be pried from Mikayla's side as EMTs crowded beside him. At some point, he wasn't sure when, the alarm had been disarmed. His father stood next to him, his hand on Noah's shoulder.

T.J. didn't offer any words, but his presence meant the world. Isaac and Eli were there, hovering just far enough he knew either one would be by his side in a heartbeat if he asked. And then there was Marianne and Gina giving enough room for Noah to breathe but there.

Seeing the EMT put an oxygen mask over Mikayla's solemn face caused a flashback. Noah's own mother had been taken from the house in the same way never to return.

Noah couldn't lose hope.

"Her vital signs are strong," one of the EMTs said.

Noah followed the gurney to the ambulance and watched as she was loaded. He was ready to climb inside when the other EMT put his hand up to stop Noah.

"I'm sorry. You can't ride back here with us."

The driver came around the side of the ambulance. "Hop in front in the passenger seat. You can ride with me."

Noah did. His family said they'd meet him there.

The ride felt like it took forever and in all the chaos Noah had forgotten to ask about Dakota. The fact that Eli had come back to the house must've meant Dakota was stabilized. So many other thoughts shot through his mind.

As soon as the ambulance arrived in the ER bay, a team wearing white coats ran out and around the back end of the vehicle.

"It might be a while before you see her, but she seems like a fighter. This is the best hospital in the region. They'll take good care of her."

"Thank you." Noah appreciated the driver's words of encouragement more than he could ever show.

Noah exited the vehicle. Out of the corner of his eye, he saw the white-coated team surround the gurney and usher her inside the automatic double glass doors. By the time he was deposited into a waiting room and fisted his first cup of coffee, his brothers and Gina had arrived.

Dale stepped into the room behind Noah's family along with Mikayla's mother.

"Any word on Dakota?" Noah immediately asked.

"He's stable. The outlook is good according to the doc." Dale kept his head bowed and wrung his hands around his cowboy hat.

"Coffee is in the corner if anyone wants a cup. It might be a long night." Each of Noah's brothers gave him a bear hug as he walked past. Gina embraced him and told him how much she liked Mikayla and that everything would work out. Even Dale offered a hug. Mikayla's mother sat quietly, waiting for news.

An hour passed as Noah paced and sipped coffee. Then two. By the third, he was ready to climb the walls.

The door to the waiting room opened and the doctor walked in. He was on the young side with serious eyes and a runner's build. "I'm Dr. Hill."

"I'm Noah Quinn." He offered a handshake. The doctor had a firm grip.

"She lost a lot of blood but her vitals are strong. She's stabilized, awake and asking for you."

"Does that mean I can go see her now?" Hope blossomed in Noah's chest.

"Yes. One at a time."

"We'll be right here, Noah. Take all the time you need," Isaac reassured.

Having his brother home was a good feeling.

Mikayla's mother stood. "I'll go make her favorite brownies."

"I bet she'd love that." Noah followed the doctor down the hall and to the only woman he could see in his future. Mikayla was propped up. Her face beamed as he walked into the room.

He thanked the doctor and then high-tailed it to her bedside.

She winced as she tried to sit up to greet him.

"Don't move." Her face was the most beautiful thing he'd seen in hours. "Don't hurt yourself."

"Jess?"

"He's in county lockup."

A knock at the door interrupted the reunion. Griff poked his head inside. "Mind if I come in?"

Noah waved his cousin inside.

"Heard the news about Dakota."

Mikayla's face twisted in confusion. "He figured Jess out, which Jess couldn't afford. He bashed Dakota in the head and left him for dead. We found him and got him to the hospital. He's stabilized now but he's had a rough road."

"Was anyone else hurt?"

"No one aside from you and Dakota." Noah looked to Griff for confirmation. Got it.

"Bode came clean. He finally returned my call when I told him about Jess."

"What was his problem?"

"He got himself wrapped up in an affair with a prominent San Antonio socialite. He was with her that night and knew if he got her name involved, her husband would come after him. Apparently, the last guy she had an affair with ended up in a box six feet under. Her husband threatened to kill her if she jumped in the sack with another man."

"That explains why he was so cryptic."

"And desperate to talk to me. Maybe he figured he could convince me that he wasn't out to hurt me." Mikayla made good sense. Noah still wanted to punch Bode in the face for keeping a secret that almost killed Mikayla.

If Bode had come clean earlier, they could've ruled him out and possibly gotten to the truth before anyone else got hurt.

"I'll leave you two alone. I thought you deserved to know first."

"Thank you, Griff."

"See you at Sunday supper?"

Noah had almost forgotten about Sunday suppers at Casa Grande. He liked the idea as long as Mikayla was game. "I'll be there if they let Mikayla go home by then and if she'll join us."

She smiled, nodded.

"Two more for dinner." Griff started toward the door. "Marianne will be overjoyed."

Griff closed the door behind him, finally leaving Mikayla and Noah alone. He had an important question to ask.

One that required him getting down on one knee.

So he did.

Right there in the hospital, next to the bed, Noah took a knee.

"What are you doing?" Mikayla covered her mouth when she gasped.

"I love you with everything I am, Mikayla Rae Johnson. There's no other woman I could love more. I want to make my intentions clear. I'm here for the long haul. I'd be honored if you'd agree to become my wife. But, I understand this might be too soon for you. I want you to know that I'll wait until you're ready. Take as much time as you need. I'm not going anywhere unless you ask me to leave."

"I love you, Noah Quinn. Marrying you would be the best first day of the rest of our lives. There's no reason for me to wait and I don't need a fancy ceremony. I'm ready to build a life together and there's no one else I'd rather spend forever with than you."

Noah stood and then kissed his future bride. His Mikayla. His future. His home.

18

EPILOGUE

Liam Quinn had been out of cell range for the past five days and had too little sleep to worry about it. Calf season kept him busier than usual when one of the ranch hands he worked with had decided to walk off the job. Rupert had said he was done shoveling shit. He preferred to mine black gold instead. With an apology, he'd hopped into his pickup and headed north toward Alaska.

More than once Rupert had said Liam could handle the entire operation on his own if need be. He'd praised Liam for caring about the CC Ranch like it was his own. Little did Rupert know Liam had more experience ranching than the owners. He liked being anonymous in Colorado. Don't get him wrong, Texas was home and always would be. Here, he wasn't T.J. Quinn's son, and that suited him just fine.

Rupert's replacement had been found almost immediately and it had only taken three days to get the greenhorn up and running. Jack Trevor might only be eighteen-years-old, but the guy was made for cattle ranching. All he'd needed was a chance to prove himself and, thanks to Rupert, Jack got his turn.

Training a greenhorn during a five-day, no-sleep work binge had left Liam more than ready to crash hard, like a rock star on tour hard. The family Liam worked for had three adult sons, all of whom arrived today, ready and able to pitch in. The cavalry had arrived.

So, when he finally showered and dropped onto bed the last thing he wanted to do was check his phone.

The damn thing kept buzzing on the nightstand, so he reached over and snatched it off. He rubbed blurry eyes that were too dry and too tired to focus. Squinting at the screen, he made out the double-digit number of texts he'd received. *Damn.* That couldn't signal good news.

As his mind snapped to several worst-case scenarios, he shoved his aggravation aside. Air squeezed out of his lungs and he broke into a cold sweat, praying everyone back home was safe. Pushing up to sitting, he blinked a few times and shook his head, trying to clear the heavy blanket of fog from his mind.

Liam immediately noticed that most of the texts came from his twin brother, Isaac. He used his thumb to scroll to the top of the messages. The first one was from weeks ago and announced that Isaac had left the service and returned home. Damn.

Reading through the texts, he learned their father had some kind of announcement worthy of getting everyone under the same roof. News that big explained why his phone had blown up over the past couple of weeks. April had started off like a rocket and seemed ready to stay true to form the entire month.

Folks who dealt with Liam on a regular basis knew his phone was the least efficient and least likely way to reach him. A person had to basically show up in the barn if he or she wanted his attention this time of year. Isaac, of all people, would know what working a cattle ranch was like as would the rest of his family.

The thought struck an unnerving chord because T.J. would know how difficult it would be for Liam to pick up and leave his job on a moment's notice. The announcement must be big, which caused a round of *What the hell*-type questions to surface.

What the hell could be so important? T.J. was too damn strong and too damn stubborn to be seriously sick. *Right?*

What the hell was T.J. up to? There weren't a ton of options that came to mind if illness could be ruled out.

And then there was the whole...*Who in the hell did T.J. think he was to make such a demand?* Liam didn't exactly have fond feelings toward his old man.

So, he thumbed down the list of texts, stopping on the one from Isaac that was a sucker punch. It read: *Hey, bro. I'm getting married. Call me back.* Followed by: *She has a kid. I'm about to be a father.*

Liam's past came crashing down around him. He threw the covers off, hopped up and started pacing. He stabbed his fingers through his hair. The pain from seven years ago was still so real, so raw and all-consuming.

Learning that his twin had a family shouldn't be a gut punch. On some level, he'd known this day would come and Isaac deserved all the happiness in the world.

So why did the air feel like it had been sucked out of the room? His lungs clawed for oxygen as he crouched low on his knees, rocking back and forth. He'd kept his emotions locked inside and buried so deep and for so long that it felt like a bomb had detonated inside him.

Damn the day at Quinnland Ranch that had taken so much from him—a day that had defined time in two measures, before Lynn's accident and after Lynn's accident. *Jesus.*

He had to remind himself to take it down a notch. Breathe. There was no amount of pain that would cause him to let his brother down.

Scrolling through the rest of the messages, Liam realized he might be too late for Isaac's wedding but not to congratulate him on his new life. Nothing would keep Liam from forcing a smile and shaking his brother's hand no matter how he felt on the inside.

KEEP READING to find out what happens when Liam returns to the ranch and meets Savannah, a woman hiding from her past. Click here.

ALSO BY BARB HAN

Don't Mess With Texas Cowboys

Texas Cowboy Justice

Texas Cowboy's Honor

Texas Cowboy Daddy

Texas Cowboy's Baby

Texas Cowboy's Bride

Texas Cowboy's Family

Cowboys of Cattle Cove

Cowboy Reckoning

Cowboy Cover-up

Cowboy Retribution

Cowboy Judgment

Cowboy Conspiracy

Cowboy Rescue

Cowboy Target

Crisis: Cattle Barge

Sudden Setup

Endangered Heiress

Texas Grit

Kidnapped at Christmas

Murder and Mistletoe

Bulletproof Christmas

For more of Barb's books, visit www.BarbHan.com.

ABOUT THE AUTHOR

Barb Han is a USA TODAY and Publisher's Weekly Bestselling Author. Reviewers have called her books "heartfelt" and "exciting."

Barb lives in Texas--her true north--with her adventurous family, a poodle mix and a spunky rescue who is often referred to as a hot mess. She is the proud owner of too many books (if there is such a thing). When not writing, she can be found exploring Manhattan, on a mountain either hiking or skiing depending on the season, or swimming in her own backyard.

Printed in Great Britain
by Amazon